Published by D A Nelson

10 9 8 7 6 5 4 3 2

www.danelsonauthor.com

ISBN: 9798431556241

All rights reserved. No part of this publication may be reproduced or transmitted in any form or by any means, electronic, mechanical, including photocopying, recording or by any information storage retrieval system without permission of the author.

This edition published by D A Nelson © 2018
The right of D A Nelson to be identified as author of this work has been asserted by her in accordance with Copyright, Designs and Patents Act 1988.

For Mum and Dad xxx

Dusting Down Alcudia

D A NELSON

Prologue

"TELL me about Aelia's necklace again!" "Oh, you don't want to hear that boring old story again, Nina." "I do! Tell me papa!"

"All right," said Antonio, his dark eyes twinkling brightly. "Once upon a time, a thousand years ago in the time of the first Roman Emperor Augustus, in the Roman town of Pollentia on the island of Mallorca, where daddy grew up, there lived a girl called Aelia. Aelia lived with her widowed father, Quintus Livius Cato, in a villa in a beautiful part of town. Quintus was the chief lawman and very important. When it came the time for his daughter to marry, he wanted only the very best man as his son-in-law, so he went on a journey to the mainland to find his only daughter a groom. But Aelia had other ideas. While her father was away, a Roman legion camped nearby and in charge of the legion was a handsome General named Marcus Scaevola. When Aelia saw Marcus for the first time, her heart fluttered and she knew that this was the man she was meant to marry. Marcus felt the same about her and began wooing the beautiful noblewoman. After several weeks of courting, Marcus asked Aelia to marry him. She didn't hesitate in saying yes – but there was one problem. Marcus had to ask Aelia's father for permission so the couple were forced to wait until he came home."

Nina's father always paused here for effect.

"Tell me what happened next!" she squealed.

Antonio smiled and continued: "On his return three months later, Mettellus was angry with his daughter. Didn't he, as her father, have the right to say who she should and should not marry? And who was this Marcus Scaevola anyway? What were his prospects? However, when he saw how much his daughter loved the dashing General, his heart melted and he gave them his blessing. The couple were very happy and began making plans for a lavish wedding in the spring. Until tragedy struck; the Emperor called Marcus back to Rome. He and his men were to go and fight the Numidians in Africa, they had been causing some trouble. It was called the Jugurthine War. Marcus managed to return to Mallorca to see Aelia before he left. He presented her with a necklace so beautiful that it took her breath away. It was made of pure gold and had the most beautiful amethysts Aelia had ever seen. He had commissioned it for their wedding day but decided to give it to her before he left for the war. He made her promise she would wear it every day until he returned to marry her."

"Why did he do that papa?" the little girl asked.

"So, she would not forget him," replied her father. "Marcus went off to war and Aelia waited and waited for him to come back. As promised, she wore the necklace every day and she never forgot him. Days, weeks, months went by and still she waited. Then word came that the General had been killed in battle. Grief-stricken, Aelia lay down on her bed, her necklace around her neck, and died right there and then of a broken heart.

"Fearful that his daughter's body would be disturbed by robbers and her necklace taken from her, Livius buried her in a secret grave. Since then, many people have tried to find it. But she had been hidden her well. To this day, no-one knows where Aelia and her necklace lie."

D A NELSON

Chapter 1

NINA flopped into her aisle seat and clipped her belt around her slim waist. Made it...just! She sat back and caught her breath, her face florid from running. She felt uncomfortably sweaty – 'glowing' as her mother would have put it – and her legs were a little shaky from the mad sprint from the taxi to the check-in desk to the terminal. She closed her eyes and breathed in deeply. In for three…out for four, just as her yoga teacher had taught her. She felt her body slough off the creeping anxiety of the last manic hour and when she opened her eyes again she was relaxed and ready for the journey ahead.

The plane was packed, but she barely noticed the chatter of her fellow passengers - holidaymakers sparkling in their new clothes and haircuts - choosing instead to drown it out by planning the days ahead. She was excited and scared and elated all at the same time. Her stomach flipped as she thought about what she had to do. It was not going to be easy and she knew she had to get a grip of her emotions if she was to carry out her mission and achieve her goal. She must not lose her head to the romance of it all…failure was just not an option.

The plane's engines whined into life, ready for take-off. Nina felt a thrill jolt through her body like a shock of electricity.

This was it…she was really going to do it.

"Ladies and gentlemen, this is your captain speaking…" And to think, Nina had nearly missed the redeye. Her alarm clock had failed to go off and had it not been for the anxious calls of her flat-mate, Gracie, she might still have been in her cosy Chelsea bedroom dreaming of Aelia's treasure. Thank God for Gracie! She was a little scatty at times, but she had never let Nina down in all the years she had known her. Nina trusted Gracie with her life. They had met when Nina moved down from Glasgow to London to take up a job at the British Museum. Gracie, fresh out of a doomed relationship with a long-haired heavy metal musician, was looking for a flat-mate; Nina, a flat. They hit it off and soon became firm friends despite Gracie's penchant for bad-boy boyfriends and cheese and strawberry jam sandwiches. Nina smiled when she thought of her and was grateful Gracie was such an early riser. Without her, Nina knew she would not have been on this flight.

She was feeling a bit more comfortable now or as comfortable as one could feel in the tight confines of 'cattle class'. The cabin crew took up their positions at the front, middle and rear to take disinterested passengers through the safety display. Nina placed her handbag under the chair at her feet as instructed and prepared herself for the flight. She had a lot to do when she landed and wanted to think things through.

"Sleep in, Dr Esposito?" a familiar voice drawled in a New York accent.

She turned to see who had spoken and was shocked to be confronted by the handsome face of a smirking Jay Reynolds.

"Dr Reynolds, how nice to see you again," she lied, quickly composing herself. She had not seen him since…since… She managed the bare minimum of a smile. "Now what is a man like you doing on a holiday flight to Mallorca? Hardly the type of place you're normally seen."

"Same reason as you, I suppose," he grinned. His soft blue eyes were startling in the sunlit cabin.

She flinched. Did he know? How could he know? A flutter of panic dipped from her chest to the pit of her stomach. She was not sure what was causing the sensation: fear that he knew what she was going to Mallorca for, or the distant memories of a nearly-begun love affair swarming into her head like an invading army of ants. She blushed.

"And what's that?" she said, voice controlled, lips tight.

"Going on holiday of course."

He sat back lazily, legs stretched out as far as they could, arms behind his blond head, studying her.

"More like a busman's holiday," he admitted. "Going to see a man about an artifact in Palma."

"Anything I should know about?" she asked coolly before she mentally punished herself for letting him think she was interested.

"Nothing you need to worry your pretty little head over, Nina, honey," he schmoozed. "It's too small for you to be interested in. I'm sure you've got much bigger fish to fry."

"And what's that supposed to mean?" She was beginning to feel the strain of being nice him. She was letting him get to her, she knew it, but she could not help herself. He was so... so...infuriating. She could not stand the man. Putting aside what he had done to her, he was just so insufferably smug. She did not know what she had seen in him all those months ago when she had thought him charming. Charming! Sickening more like.

"Just that I'm sure you'll be too busy enjoying your holiday, topping up your tan and supping the local vino to be bothered about work," he answered with a smirk.

A scowl brushed her face. She opened her mouth to retaliate, thought better of it and turned away. He was nothing to her… nothing. He did not exist. She did not have to look at him or speak to him if she did not want to. She leant down, fished her novel out of her bag and began to read. She would just ignore him and he would go away. She could hear him chuckling from the other side of the aisle and twisted her body away from him.

The engines of the plane revved to an almost deafening roar. "Oh, looks like we're for the off," he said loudly, settling more into his seat.

No shit Sherlock, she thought and fought the urge to say it. Lips pursed she looked at her book. She would not speak to him again. She had too much to think about. He was just an irritant she would have to put up with for the duration of the flight and then she would be rid of him. Even though her eyes were fixed on the words on the page, the ones she had read at least twice, she knew full well he was trying to catch her attention. He did not say anything, but she could feel the heat of his eyes on her neck, willing her to turn around. She tried to ignore him, but he was making her skin prickle. She put down the book and tried to look like she was concentrating on the safety talk. She turned.

"What?" she asked briskly.

He laughed.

"Hope you have a good holiday," he said quietly, "…and, if there is anything you want me to get for you, just let me know."

"I don't think so, somehow…"

He grinned: "Be careful now. Don't do anything I wouldn't do…like losing an artifact!"

Before she could answer him, Jay lay back in his chair and closed his eyes, haughtily signalling the conversation was over. She scowled at him. That man was impossible. He was always impossible. The last time she had seen him was six months ago in Venice when she was on the hunt for a rare Roman perfume bottle to add to the collection at the British Museum. They had been staying at the same hotel, met in the hotel bar and she had been flattered by the attentions of this interesting and handsome man who shared her interest in antiquities. Then she had stupidly allowed herself to relax and she told him she was there on a buying trip. He was too and before they went to their separate rooms they agreed to meet the following afternoon to compare buys. The next morning, thinking no more of it, she contacted the seller, turned up at the agreed meeting place and found that Jay Reynolds had pipped her at the post. He had offered a ludicrous amount over the asking price and snatched the bottle for a private collection. Exasperated, furious with Reynolds and herself, she immediately returned to London empty-handed to explain to her museum bosses how an experienced archaeologist like her could be gazumped by the notorious Dr Jay Reynolds. She glanced over at him then angrily pushed back into her chair. He was ignoring her now. He was... insufferable!

The rest of the flight passed uneventfully. Breakfast was served along with the morning papers, and Nina soon found herself lost in the day's news. Reynolds continued to lie against the back of his seat, eyes closed, appearing to sleep, and stayed that way for the entire journey, leaving Nina in peace to think about the days ahead.

She was flying out to Mallorca to try to unravel a mystery that had fascinated her since childhood and thwarted generations of archaeologists before her: the whereabouts of the legendary Aelia's Treasure, a necklace of fabulous proportions and incomparable beauty. Reputedly forged by the best goldsmiths in Rome, decorated with the biggest and brightest amethysts, the necklace's current resting place was a mystery. Nina pulled a tattered leather-bound notebook from her bag and, keeping it out of Jay's eye-line, opened it. Written by the eminent archaeologist, Joseph Harper, in the late 1970s, she was positive it held enough clues to would lead her to the necklace. Just like Harper before her, she was sure of its existence even if the rest of the world was not. Harper had been slated over his fruitless search and that was something Nina was going to put right.

The handwriting was clear and firm; strong prose written by a strong personality:

3rd September, 1979

I've returned to Alcudia once again. Mary was angry that I wanted to 'waste more money' as she put it but as I explained to her, my search would give her and Jack a holiday abroad. She calmed down when I told her I had booked us in to the best hotel in C'an Pastilla. There's a swimming pool and night entertainment. Just what she and the boy need.

I am hoping to drop in on Juan Sebastian Gomez. As chief curator of museums and artifacts for the island authority he may be able to provide a greater insight into the legend of the necklace. He, of all people, must have some thoughts on the matter as to whether it is still buried on the island. And if so, where it might be? I hope this is not just another wasted journey...

How pertinent that was to her own trip. She had come into

possession of Harper's notebook after his death three months ago, at the age of 81. His widow had gifted his papers, artifacts and personal belongings to the British Museum. There the notebook had lain in a drawer for a couple of weeks before Nina had accidentally stumbled over it during research for another project. Her heart leapt as she recognised its significance. After years of watching Harper on television and reading everything he had ever wrote, here was his own notes in his own hand on the one project he had failed to complete: the search for Aelia's necklace. She went to her boss.

George Rayburn sighed when his best archaeologist and researcher bounced into his office, Harper's notebook in her hand. It was the end of the week, he was tired and the last thing he needed was Nina Esposito in his office with another mission she "just had to go on".

"This is a sign, George," Nina gushed, placing the notebook carefully on his desk, "a sign. I was meant to find this notebook. It was hidden under a whole load of journals Joseph Harper's widow had donated to the museum. How long has this been lying there for? Didn't anyone check for gems like this? If I hadn't been looking through them it might never have to come to light. Well, at least not for many years. I was meant to find it and I'm meant to find Aelia's treasure. You've got to let me go to Mallorca to search for it. You have to!"

"I see you've found it then," he said quietly.

And that is the worst thing that could have happened, his expression said. Nina had a reputation of being a bit of a Pitbull when she got something between her teeth. She was not one to let go of anything easily.

"I can't believe my luck. Harper's notebook! That man is a god to me. More than a god! Like Indiana Jones - "

"I was going to talk to you about this - "

"Travelling the world uncovering new civilizations. Oh, I've worshipped him since I was a girl…"

"But I haven't had the chance…"

"I read all of his books. He's responsible for me becoming interested in Ancient Rome! You could say he's responsible for me coming to work here."

"Miss Esposito! Sit."

She threw herself into a chair, clasped her hands on her knees and stared at him expectantly, her eyes shining.

George did not seem to know where to start. What he had to tell Nina was explosive. He was straight with her. "For your information, we did look through the notebooks and that was looked at, but we just don't have the resources to follow through. Not yet."

He continued: "Look, this is a long shot, but Nina a contact of mine in Madrid has uncovered papers written by an 11th century priest known as Padre Cornelius. They talk about the legend of a Roman noblewoman being buried with a fantastic treasure close to Pollentia. There are only a few lines, but he could be talking about Aelia. As you are aware, everything we do know about her comes from Mallorcan folk tales and stories, so it's rather a leap of faith."

"Yes, but this might be the first time we've ever found written evidence that the necklace might actually have existed," she said, barely able to breathe.

And that would mean Joseph Harper's theories were right. She knew it!

"Well, we don't know for sure…" George began.

"But, surely with the help of Joseph Harper's diary and Padre Cornelius papers, we've got a good chance of finding it. You've got to let me go to Mallorca," she said, her voice quick with excitement, her hands shaking with nerves. "I've got to find it. It's got to be me." She stood up. "Please say you'll send me. You've got to let me go, George."

"Hold on a minute," he said, "I've got to get the permission of the Board before I can let you go anywhere. You know what they're like. They may think it's all a waste of time and money. Let's face it, if Joseph Harper failed to find it, what makes you think you will?"

"If what you say is true, then there's a tomb somewhere in northern Mallorca that's just waiting to be found. And I can find it, George." She was determined she was going. "I have to do this. I have to do this for Joseph Harper, I have to do this for the museum and most of all I have to do this for myself."

George looked steadily at her. "I'll try my best to persuade them," he said.

Three agonising days passed before the Board met to take the decision. It was all Nina could do to stop herself from emailing the members personally to plead with them. As they met in the museum's huge boardroom to discuss the proposal, she waited outside. She hoped and prayed their decision would go her way. She begged every god (ancient and modern) she could think of to let the Board come out in her favour. Yet when the meeting finally ended, when they finally spilled out of the boardroom, when their eyes would not meet hers, she knew what was coming next. George broke the bad news to her. "Why won't they sanction the trip?" she snapped. "Are they mad? Don't they know what this will do for the reputation of the museum? This could be the find of the century."

"I know, Nina, you don't have to tell me..." he began.

She grabbed him by the shoulders and looked him straight in the eye.

"You've got to persuade them to let me go." She was having difficulty controlling her disappointment, stopping the tears that threatened to fall. "I've got everything else I need. All the documentation is there. Harper's notes, all the clues are there. I'm sure of this, George. I will find the necklace."

"Nina," he said, releasing himself from her grip. "I tried everything I could but they were adamant. They said they needed firmer evidence that the necklace every existed before they would pay for you to go and look for it. I'm sorry. Now, if you'll excuse me, I've got another meeting to go to."

He started to quickly walk away, his feet pit-patting on the tiled floor. She caught up with him.

"Have you any idea how important this is to me?"

He gave her a sympathetic, knowing look, the type her mother gave her when her first boyfriend finished with her at the age of 12. This time, there was no amount of chocolate digestives that were going to put this one right.

"I know your late father used to tell you the story of the necklace when you were little. I know how special finding it would be to you," George said, "but my hands are tied."

"Are they?" she snapped, anger flashing in her eyes. "Or are you just too chicken to stand up for your staff?"

She was standing still now, hands on hips. Defiant.

"Now hold on just a minute!" He turned to face her, his nostrils flared with irritation. The colour rose in his cheeks. "If the Board says no, it's no. I can't do anything else." He strode angrily away, head high in indignation.

"Well, I can," she whispered to herself.

Back in her office she booked two weeks holiday and a plane ticket to Palma. If the museum would not back her, she would back herself. Armed with Harper's notebook and with her late father's tale ringing in her head, Nina was confident she would break this mystery once and for all. How could she fail? The story of Aelia and the necklace is real, she said to herself, and I'm going to prove it.

Chapter 2

PALMA Airport was jammed with pasty-faced tourists dragging an assortment of bags and fractious children in and out of luggage collection. As the mothers soothed their whining offspring, the fathers, faces tight with anxiety, made their way to the scrum of the luggage belt where the crowd bottle-necked to grab their cases. Nina, hated this part and stood off to one side until most of the people disappeared. Then she retrieved her case from the moving belt.

She looked around, searching for the tall silhouette of Jay Reynolds but the treasure hunter was nowhere in sight. She had not seen him since they disembarked and was pleased she at least would not have to face him again. Nina unclipped her suitcase's long handle and, with a shake of her long dark hair, strode towards Arrivals. She was on her way.

Nina had opted to stay with her father's sister, Aunt Rosita, and her family in the old town of Alcudia where they owned a café and hostel. Nina had called them a couple of days before and, with a shriek of delight, her aunt insisted she stay with her. They arranged to pick her up at the airport so it was with excitement that Nina stepped out through the swing doors.

Arrivals was a colourful sea of bustling travellers and airport officials and it took Nina some time to make out the familiar black hair and comfortable curves of her favourite aunt. Rosita was a tiny woman, but what she lacked in height she made up for in personality.

"Nina! NINA!" Rosita called. "Has she seen us? Did she hear me?"

Rosita's daughter, Carmel, was practically holding her mother back from climbing over the barrier the smaller woman was that excited. Rosita had to make do with waving frantically and wringing her hands with joy.

"How could she not?" Carmel sighed, "I think the whole airport heard you, mamma."

Nina pushed through the stream of people to the barrier and was greeted with hugs and kisses from her aunt and cousin.

"My goodness, little Nina!" Rosita cried. "You're so grown up now. The last time I saw you you were just a young girl. Now look at you, you're a woman."

"Aunt Rosita, I was 19 the last time you saw me. Hardly a baby," Nina answered her in perfect Catalan and laughed. "But Carmel! Is that you? The last time I saw you, you were…"

"I know," smiled Carmel, "fourteen going on forty!"

"I hardly recognised you," Nina laughed. She looked around. "Where's Uncle Javier and Jaume?"

Rosita rolled her eyes.

"In the car, listening to football on the radio. Can you believe it? Our Nina comes to visit and they want to hear how their team is doing in the league! Men!" Rosita sighed.

"If you're all here who's running the café?"

"No-one. We closed specially to come and pick you up," Carmel said. "Mamma insisted."

Nina shot Rosita a look of surprise. Her aunt merely shrugged.

"Well how often is it that my favourite niece comes to visit?" she said with a smile.

"I'm your only niece," Nina gently reminded her.

Rosita patted her on her cheek.

"And you get more like your late father every day," she said sadly, her eyes misting. Then: "What are we all doing standing here? I've got a lovely lunch planned for you. Come on! Let's go and get those football daft men of mine!"

Although it was only 10.30 in the morning, Nina still felt a blast of heat from the Mallorcan sun as soon as she followed her aunt and cousin outside. The sun's rays bounced off the black tarmac and intensified the feeling leading her to fan herself with a hand. Squinting in the bright light, Nina looked around for her uncle and cousin.

"Lost something?" Jay Reynolds was suddenly at her side. He had the loopy grin that got Nina's hackles up right away.

"Just looking for my uncle," she replied steadily. "Haven't you got somewhere to be?"

"Nina! Don't be so rude!" her aunt chided in heavily accented English. Rosita smiled and held out her hand to him. "Who is this lovely man? Is he a friend?" Jay grinned broadly and before Nina could say anything, he turned his full attention – and devastating charm - on Rosita and Carmel.

"Enchante," he said taking the older woman's hand and kissing it. "That's what you say here in Mallorca isn't it?"

Rosita giggled. Nina rolled her eyes.

"They do that in France!" she hissed, but he didn't seem to hear.

"Hello," Rosita giggled. "I'm Nina's Aunt Rosita, this is my daughter, Carmel...and you are?"

"Jay Reynolds, a colleague of Nina's. I'm surprised she hasn't spoken of me before."

"Nina never introduces us to any of her charming men friends," said Rosita pointedly. "What are you doing here? Holidaying?"

"No, I've got some business to attend to in Palma," he replied. "Then it's back to New York for me."

"New York? In America?" Carmel gasped. She looked impressed.

Nina rolled her eyes again, exasperated.

"Yes, I work there." He smiled at Carmel.

She gushed: "I've never been to America. I'd love to go some day."

"Perhaps you can come out and visit me sometime. I could show you around," he said then shot Nina a smug look.

Nina's lips tightened. Stay-away-from-my-family, her eyes growled.

Carmel returned the smile: "That would be lovely."

"So," her mother interrupted, "will you get to see the island while you're here? Are you planning to come to the north side?"

He sighed.

"I'm not sure. I have a business meeting with my contact in Palma and then I'll probably head off home."

Rosita looked shocked.

"Oh, no no no!" she said, "you must experience more of our lovely island than that. The Sant Jaume Fiesta starts tomorrow in Alcudia. You can't miss it. It's fantastic, you would enjoy it. We'd love you to come and visit. "

"Aunt Rosita," Nina began, horrified. She didn't want that man anywhere near her. "I'm sure Dr Reynolds has better things to do with his time."

"Dr Reynolds? You're a doctor?" she shot an 'I'm impressed' look at Nina. She grimaced back. "How wonderful," Aunt Rosita winked at her niece.

She leaned into him and whispered conspiratorially: "You will definitely have to visit us now and tell us all about your work."

Jay seemed genuinely delighted.

"I'd love to," he replied.

"Hey Rosita! Hurry up!" The heavy frame of Uncle Javier was half in, half out of the car he had driven round to the front of the terminal. "I'm hungry. I want my lunch."

"Javi, can't you see I'm busy? I'll be there in a minute!" Rosita shouted. Sighing, she turned back to Jay. "We own the Café Bolo in Alcudia Old Town." She patted his arm. "Please come." She winked at him now. "Then you can tell me all about how you met Nina."

"With pleasure!" he said with relish, grinning from ear to ear like a six-foot Cheshire cat. "I'd love to tell you all about it. It's really an interesting story, isn't it Nina?"

"Is it?" Nina said through thinned lips, ice in her voice. "Aunt, hadn't we better go?"

"In a minute," Rosita said. She patted Jay on the arm. "You will come, won't you?"

He nodded. "I wouldn't miss it for the world."

"Rosita!" Uncle Javier sounded more urgent.

A police car was hovering nearby threatening a parking ticket.

"Everybody always wants me," Rosita sighed. "Coming!" She shouted back to her anxious spouse. "Goodbye Dr Reynolds. It was very nice to meet you." She shook his hand. "I hope we'll see you soon."

She turned and trotted over to the waiting car, dragging Nina's case behind her. Carmel followed, leaving Nina with Jay.

"You have a nice family, Nina," Jay said. He seemed amused by her obvious discomfort. "I'm looking forward to meeting the rest of them."

She shot him a look that would have withered a lesser man.

"Don't even think about it," she hissed. "Stay away from me and my family."

"Why not? I could do with some good old Mallorcan hospitality," he teased.

"You know why not. You stole that artifact from me."

"It was business, Nina, nothing personal, you know that," he said. "Are you sure you're not all uppity for any other reason? Like maybe you haven't totally gotten over me."

"And maybe your huge ego can't understand that there was nothing to get over!" She snapped. Huffing, she pushed past him and followed her family to the car, not looking back to see whether he was still watching or not. As she reached the car, Rosita stuck her head out of the window and shouted, "Remember: Café Bolo in Alcudia Old Town!"

"I won't forget!" he called after her and waved back.

Jay remained standing in the hot morning sun while Nina squeezed into the back of her uncle's small car. There was not much space next to Carmel and Jaume, but as the car drove off, Nina managed to twist around and see if he was still there. He waved. Huffing again, she spun around, and folded her arms across her chest in annoyance. Damn, he caught her looking.

"Why did you invite him to Alcudia, Aunt Rosita?" Nina asked when the hateful man was finally out of sight.

"Why not? He seems like a really nice man." "He's not. Appearances are deceptive in his case," grumbled Nina.

"Oh, I don't think so. He's got such nice eyes."

"You can't tell what a person's like by his eyes, mamma," Jaume interjected.

"That's how your mother chose me!" Javier chuckled. Everyone laughed and the tension melted away.

The journey to Alcudia took an hour but it was one that Nina had always enjoyed. As they raced along Mallorca's only motorway to the north, she caught up on family news whilst reacquainting herself with the mountainous beauty of the island. It had been a long time since she had been to this part of the world and she wondered why she had not come back sooner. What was she saying? She knew only full well why. His name was Roberto. She was 19 when she fell for the Latin charms of Roberto Hernandez. He had been this 22-year-old dark-eyed, dark haired, muscular God of the Sea who had been working for her Uncle Javi as a waiter during the summer. From the moment she first set eyes on him, the teenage Nina was smitten. She had pursued him quietly, spending hours sitting in the café mooching over the handsome object of her affections. He, in turn, was flattered that this lovely girl was showing an interest in him. They became friends first, but, before either of them realised what was happening, love sent them dizzily into each other's arms. They spent the rest of the summer glued to each other. Where you would find one, the other would be close by. He was her first love and swore she was his. She thought it would last forever; that they would grow old with each other and in her head, she began to plan their wedding and the future life together. What she was not prepared for the shock that came next. It hit her like a sledge hammer… it was over.

It was Roberto who ended it, but he did not have the guts to say it to her face. Instead, he waited until she had flown home to go back to university. He had promised to call and write, but nothing came. At first, she tried to dismiss it as his being busy. Then she tried to get in touch with him, but he was never available to take her calls. Then, two weeks after she had returned to Britain, a letter arrived telling her it was over, that he had met someone else. She was sick with shock. How could he? What had she done? She picked over everything he had ever said, everything he had done to see if there were any clues, any way she could have seen this coming. There was none. She never could find an explanation, a reason, for his behaviour and her heartbreak had cast a long shadow over her life for many years afterwards.

Nina had not really given Roberto much thought on the way over, but as the car drew closer to Alcudia, a bitter-sweet sadness descended on her as she remembered the good times they had together. She wondered what he was doing now and if she would bump into him while she was here. She wondered if she wanted to bump into him. He had, after all, unceremoniously dumped her for someone else. She was annoyed with herself for even thinking about him. That meant she still had some feelings for him and that was something she was not comfortable with. It's better to let sleeping dogs lie, she told herself. It was a long time ago and best forgotten. She had to focus. She had a lot of work to do if she ever had a hope of finding Aelia's Treasure and she did not have time to mooch over her past or anyone in it. But as she silently scolded herself she knew her return to Alcudia was going to open up a lot of feelings that had lain dormant for years. She knew she was on the verge of an emotional rollercoaster because, despite it being nearly ten years since she had last seen him with numerous boyfriends in between, Nina had never forgotten her first love. Frightened of how she would react if she met him again, she hoped to hell their paths would not cross. That was a blow to her self-esteem she could do without taking again.

"Nearly there!" Aunt Rosita shouted cheerily from the front seat of the car. "Oh Nina! I've made your favourite for lunch."

"Sobrassada? You've made me Sobrassada? But it's not January!" Nina was delighted.

She loved the tangy Spanish sausages, roasted over the fire and served with fresh vegetables. Her mouth watered at the prospect of tucking into a plateful of these delicious treats.

"Of course, it's Sobrassada!" Aunt Rosita was beaming. "I know it's a bit out of season, but I thought I would get them in especially for you. I know you love them so much," she added.

"I love everything you cook, Aunt Rosita.".

The car drew up to a set of lights and right ahead Nina could see the familiar sandy-coloured ramparts of the old medieval city walls. On one corner, the Sant Jaume Church loomed over the small town, standing guard against the world's evils. Its huge round stained-glass window gazed out over the dry Mallorcan landscape, ever watchful for signs of wrongdoing. Behind the strong walls, Nina knew there was a charming little town with narrow streets and rows of ancient houses standing shoulder to shoulder with their neighbour. She had loved this place since she was a child and her heart gave a little leap with excitement. She would find Aelia's treasure, she resolved. As they passed the church, Nina looked up at its beautiful glass window for divine inspiration. Please let me find her, she whispered. The sun sparkled off of the many tiny coloured panes of glass, winking at her as if someone up there was letting her know God was with her. She smiled to herself. Was this a sign? She felt sure it was.

Aunt Rosita and Uncle Javier's café was all closed up as they walked from the car. It hadn't changed a bit. The vivid green of the door and window frames contrasted beautifully with the soft sandy tones of the brickwork. Green chairs and tables were stacked neatly underneath bright red and white striped awnings; the familiar chalkboard declaring the day's specials was still nailed at the door and Nina was delighted her family had left in place the ancient metal cigarette advertising board at the corner. Rosita unlocked the glass paned door and ushered her in enthusiastically. The cool tiled interior was also how she remembered it and, as she ran her hand across the smooth wooden bar, she was taken back to all the summers she had spent there, ordering Cokes for her and her cousins. Rosita guided her to the back, ordering Uncle Javier, Carmel and Jaume to stoke up the old stove in the kitchen for lunch.

"I've given you our nicest guest room," Aunt Rosita explained as Nina followed her up the bright stairwell. Her family rented out rooms above the café during the summer and Nina was relieved they still had a room for her. It was at the top of the house, away from the other guests, with a bathroom across the landing. It overlooked the town square, giving Nina a perfect view to people-watch without being seen. Nina placed her suitcase on the floor and surveyed her new home. An old metal double bed decked out in a hand-embroidered bed set took up most of the room. At the netted window, an ancient dressing table sat just waiting to be filled with her things.

"Make yourself at home Nina," her aunt said. "Lunch will be in half an hour if you want a little time to freshen up."

"Thank you, Aunt Rosita," Nina said, suddenly tired from her journey. "I'll be down shortly. I just want to change into fresh clothes first."

"No hurry. I'll see you downstairs," replied her aunt as she closed the door behind her.

Alone at last, Nina lay down on the bed and closed her eyes. Outside, she could hear the familiar sound of villagers going about their business, tourists chatting merrily to each other and the local 'Mafiosi' - as a group of elderly men who habitually sat in the square outside were fondly known - debating the merits of some footballer or other. The scent of fresh sea air and wild flowers wafted through the open windows and, for the first time in ages, she felt herself coming alive. Then it came to her, a smell so tantalisingly wicked that her nostrils strained for more and her taste buds burst into life. She sat up and sniffed again, making sure her nose had not fooled her. Yes, she was sure she was right. She stood up, yanked off her jacket and ran to the door. Freshening up could wait. She had Sobrassada to eat!

The family was already sitting chatting happily around the huge kitchen table when she entered and realised, with a small pang of sadness, just how much she had missed them. Since she had been a very small child, Nina and her parents had returned every year to Mallorca to visit their family and enjoy the famous island hospitality. Her mother had kept up the tradition following the death of her husband and, when she was old enough, Nina continued to come over on her own…. until she met Roberto. The break-up had hit her so badly, she stopped coming. That was a mistake, she realized.

Nina sat down beside the huge girth of her uncle and smiled as he passed her a glass of local wine. I'm going to make sure that no man ever stops me seeing my family in future, she vowed to herself. I won't leave it for ten years to visit here ever again. The meal passed quickly as the family tucked into the hot greasy sausages and laughed and joked together. Nina learned that her cousins were doing well for themselves; Jaume had just finished studying to become a vet and his older sister, Carmel, was working as a temporary lecturer in English at the university in Palma. She had just heard she was being taken on in a permanent position.

"Which is perfect timing," said Carmel, "considering I'm getting married next year."

"Married?" Nina was delighted. "Oh, Carmel, that's great news. Who's the lucky man?"

"His name is Christophe. He's a pharmacist. He lives in Palma and he's lovely," her cousin replied a little bashfully.

"Well? Let's see the ring!"

Carmel shyly extended her left hand. It was a beautiful diamond solitaire set on a band of gold. Nina hugged her cousin tightly. She was genuinely pleased for her, although a little envious. It had been a long time since she herself had been in love. She wondered sadly if it would ever be her turn.

Nina looked around at her family and smiled. Who needed a man when she had all these?

Later, as she was helping Rosita with the washing up, her aunt asked her how she was.

"It's been a long time," Rosita said, "too long. We understand why you stopped coming, but don't you think it's time you put the past behind you and started living again?"

"I'm fine, Aunt Rosita," Nina replied busily drying a glass, "and what do you mean 'started living again'? I live. I have my job, I have great friends and I have a life." "Do you really?" her aunt asked. "When we brought you here, I saw that look in your eyes."

"What look?"

"The look of pain! He's still here in your heart, isn't he?" she asked jabbing Nina in the chest.

"Ow! Who is?"

"That boy. Roberto!"

"I hardly think about him now. He is nothing to me."

"Really? I think you still love him. Just a little bit."

"No," Nina replied wondering if she was lying to herself as well as her aunt, "that was over a long time ago. He left me for someone else, remember? How could I still love a man like that?"

"Hmmmm."

"Why did you have to bring up Roberto, anyway? It's not like I'm ever going to see him again anyway, is it?" Nina asked. She desperately hoped the answer would be negative.

"Well, he still lives around here and…" Rosita began.

"And? What is it you're not telling me Aunt Rosita?" Fear gripped her heart and refused to let go.

"Well, he's…well he…"

"Out with it!" Don't tell me he works here, she thought. I should have checked. I was so busy rushing over here, I forgot to ask. I should have asked. Maybe I can find a hotel room somewhere else in the town…

"He supplies Javi with some of his wines. It's nothing. He only comes in sometimes. You won't see him, I promise." Rosita shrugged as she washed the last of the plates and placed them on the drying rack.

"How could you do that when you know what he did to me?" It was out before Nina could stop it. She clamped her hand over her mouth. "I'm sorry, I shouldn't have said that. It's none of my business."

"You're right, it is none of your business," replied her aunt, but Nina could see from the sparkle in her eyes that she was not angry with her. "But it is business. Javi needed a new supplier, Roberto's prices were good so we went with him."

Then she added: "He's not due to come for a few days. You won't have to see him."

Good, thought Nina as she took a plate and dried it, good.

The afternoon passed uneventfully. Nina unpacked and then joined her family downstairs in the café. Now open, the little business had already attracted a number of tourists and Nina was delighted to help Javier and Rosita behind the bar. She was surprised at how quickly she remembered how to pull a pint and before she knew it she was back into the old swing of things, working as a barmaid like she had been born to do the job.

By dinner time, Nina's feet hurt and she was glad when Rosita called her through to help set the table for their evening meal. As she cooked paella Rosita sang old Mallorcan ballads and Nina joined in the parts she remembered. The table laid, the café closed for an hour, the family gathered around the table, all excitedly chattering and catching up with Nina's more recent history. It felt like she had never left.

Dinner was over within half an hour and they sat drinking wine, enjoying the peace before the evening rush. This is just what I needed, thought Nina as she took another sip. I'd forgotten what a real tonic this lot was!

Her thoughts were interrupted by a loud banging on the front door. The family turned as one, Uncle Javier half out of his seat.

"Who's that? Don't they know we're closed?" said Aunt Rosita.

They heard the front door squeak open and footsteps filtered through. Javier took a few steps and peered out into the café.

"Hello? Anyone home?" A man's voice could be heard. "Hello?"

"I'll go and see who it is," Uncle Javier said as he strode out. "I'll get rid of them."

There was a muffled conversation and then sounds of welcome. Nina leaned over to Jaume.

"Any idea who it is?" she asked.

He shrugged and looked towards the door. It wasn't long before they found out. Within seconds of her asking the question, Javier strode through the kitchen door with his arm around…

"Roberto!" Nina gasped.

God, he looks great, she thought absently smoothing down her hair.

"Nina!" He smiled widely, his eyes shining brightly with the genuine joy of seeing her again. "I heard you were coming back."

"Roberto," Aunt Rosita's hostess mode came into being. "Come and join us. Have you eaten? Would you like some wine?"

She nudged Jaume to move up and make space.

Roberto did not seem to hear her. He could not take his eyes off Nina.

"Roberto? Roberto! Have a seat," Rosita said firmly. "There's enough time later for catching up. Javier, get Roberto some wine, will you?"

"So, how've you been?" Roberto asked as he sat down next to Nina.

She suddenly felt shy. Her stomach was in knots and her head was racing. Why was he here? Why now? Had he come to see her? She didn't know what to think. She remembered only too well the pain of separation from him, all the hurt their break-up had caused. She did not want to see him, be around him right now, but could not leave without being rude. She was rooted to the spot. Her family had gone to a lot of trouble to put this meal together, they had even shut down the café for the morning, she could not walk out on them now. She was stuck.

"Fine, and you?" was all she could say. Her throat was tight, words sounded strangled, constricted.

"Great. I'm working for myself now as a vintner. Been doing it for five years. It's good." He sipped his wine. "Javier, this wine is magnificent. Is it one of mine?"

Nina's uncle smiled. "Roberto, you know there's no wine-maker even matches your father!" He replied. "No, this has come from your family's vineyard."

"Glad to hear you're keeping the old man in business. Have you seen him lately?" Roberto asked accepting a plate of paella from Rosita.

"Spoke to him the other week. He's well," Javier replied. "He's asking after you."

"Is he now?" Roberto said.

Nina detected a slight hardness in his voice. She looked at him quizzically. Roberto caught her drift right away.

"Small family rift," he said and dropped the subject. "So, tell me about you. What have you been doing these past ten years?"

After dinner, Nina jumped to help Rosita with the dishes. She did not want to stay around Roberto any longer than was necessary and the distraction of scrubbing the plates would help her focus on the real reason she was here. Up to her elbows in suds, Nina tried to block out the sound of Roberto's voice chatting amiably to her uncle, a voice that was once so dear to her, but had caused her so much pain.

"Are you all right?" her aunt whispered at her side, expertly drying and putting away the dishes.

Nina managed a small smile.

"It's just a bit strange seeing him again, that's all," she whispered back.

"I know what you mean." Rosita picked up large knife and began to dry. She suddenly smiled. "Hey, Nina, if he ever gives you trouble again," she said in a low voice so the others wouldn't hear. "You can always cut off his cojones!" She brandished the knife and gave it a downward swipe.

Nina giggled. She could always rely on Rosita to make her smile.

Nina was so engrossed, she barely noticed Roberto standing up to leave. He actually had to walk over to her and touch her on the shoulder before she was aware anything was happening.

"Nina, may I have a word?" he asked quietly, "in private?"

Rosita sprang into action. "Don't mind us," she said, "we've got to go and get the café ready for opening." She ushered her family out of the kitchen. "Come on everyone. Out! We've got work to do."

They exited merrily, each exchanging quizzical looks with Nina who stood at the sink feeling awkward and wishing that the ground would open up and swallow her.

Aunt Rosita called back: "We'll just be through here if you need us, Nina."

Alone at last, Roberto drew closer to Nina. She moved away, unwilling to allow him into her personal space. He was not going there again.

"What do you want Roberto?" she asked, chin tilted up, looking directly into his eyes. "I'm busy. I've got a lot of things to do."

"So, hurry up? Is that what you're saying?" he asked sounding a little hurt.

She shrugged.

"Oh Nina. I just wanted say sorry for the way I treated you all those years ago. It was terrible of me and I'm sorry."

She looked away and sighed. How did she reply to that? She wanted to tell him, let him know, of all the pain and anguish she had suffered, all the longing for him, pining for him, but good sense prevailed. He did not care then, so why should he care now? He only wanted to salve his guilty conscience that was all. He wanted her forgiveness so he would feel better about it all, but there was no point in digging up the past.

"It was a long time ago, Roberto. Forget about it." Her eyes met his again. "I know I have."

"I know, but when I heard you were coming back, I wanted to see you to ask your forgiveness properly," he began. His eyes dropped to the floor. "I'm sorry, Nina. We were so far apart. It was never going to work. We… I should have known that."

He paused then continued: "I know I can't ask nor expect anything from you, but I wondered if we could at least be friends?" He extended his hand. "Please?"

Nina looked at this man standing sheepishly before her and, for the first time in ages, did not know what to do. Almost a decade had passed since they had split up and she could see no real reason, nor had a valid excuse other than her own feelings, as to why they could not be friends. If she refused, she would look petty and childish. If she agreed, what would it really cost her? Nothing really: just the exchange of a few pleasantries while she was here. She took his hand and shook it. She would probably not see him again after this anyway, so had nothing to lose by acting graciously. Her Scottish mother had drummed good manners into her from very early childhood and she was not going to let her down now.

Roberto smiled. "As my friend, would you like to join me for the Sant Jaume Fiesta celebrations tonight?" Nina grimaced. "My brother, Santos - you remember him, don't you? - owns the bar around the corner. He's having a party. Would you like to come?"

"I don't know, Roberto. I've only just arrived," she began. "I've got a lot of things on."

She was feeling uncomfortable and part of her wanted to run away.

He looked disappointed, misunderstood her meaning.

"Don't worry about Rosita and Javier, they will be busy with the café. I'll square it with them. Leave it to me." He smiled. "Please come. I'd love to take you."

"It's not that...it's just...well I'd feel weird. I've not seen Santos since...."

"It's okay, I understand. This would just be two friends having a drink together," he assured her. "No strings. No expectations." He grinned, the dimples on his cheeks springing to life. "If you don't have a good time, I'll bring you straight back home. I promise."

He added: "I'm just asking you to join me for one drink, Nina, that's all. It's my way of apologizing."

She was unsure, did not want to go, but could not think of a good enough excuse to get out of it.

"All right," she said quietly. "But, just the one and then I'm going home."

Chapter 3

JOSEPH Harper's Diary - 4th September, 1979

Juan Sebastian Gomez was not as helpful as he could be. I met up with him this afternoon while Mary and Jack went souvenir hunting in Palma. Senor Gomez claims that many people have tried to find the last resting place of Aelia, but none have found it. He said they weren't even sure if she ever existed. Many people thought her a figment of the popular imagination, a story handed down the ages to make men sick with greed as they fought each other to find her. I told him I thought she did exist and that I meant to find her and her necklace. He laughed. It was then I knew he would be of no further use to me.

Tomorrow, I will hire a car and drive the family up to Alcudia. What I do know is that Aelia is reputed to have been a noblewoman who lived in Pollentia which, we think, was on the outskirts of the modern town. Locals believe her to be buried in the countryside, some miles away. I believe a verse in the Alcudian folk song, 'My Lady of the Morning,' may hold vital clues to the whereabouts of the burial site:

My Lady did not wake one morning,
She did not see the day was dawning,

They took her and they laid her down in a chosen meadow fair.
My Lady slept a dreamless sleep,
Her beauty they did let her keep,
They took her and they laid her down betwixt her favourite places.

Does this song relate to Aelia? Does the beauty relate to her fairness or are they talking about the necklace? Where is the chosen meadow and why was she laid betwixt her favourite places? Maybe I will see these places when I go there tomorrow…

Nina lay in a bubble bath for an hour trying to read Harper's battered diary, but her mind was not really on it. For the first time in ages, she felt excited and scared about seeing a man, going out with him, enjoying his company. She could not remember the last time she had gone on date, although she was unsure as she could actually call going out with Roberto a 'date'. And then there was the problem of going out with an ex, especially one who had dumped her all those years ago. She did not know how to feel about it: on one hand she was still angry and hurt at his tawdry treatment of her; on the other she knew she still found him dangerously attractive. Was this really such a good idea? Oh, be quiet, she scolded herself. The last thing you want, Nina Esposito, is to become involved again, particularly with a man who already left you once. This is only one friend going out with another…that is all. The flutter in her stomach proved that it wasn't.

Rosita and Javier had been surprisingly quiet when she told them a little while later that she was attending the Festa party with Roberto. Javier had said nothing, merely smiled at her. Rosita had given her a hug and told her to enjoy herself, but neither of them had commented further. The only thing they wanted to know was did Nina want anything else to eat before she went out. Nina politely declined. She was too nervous to consume anything else. Besides, she had to get ready and wanted to give herself plenty of time to look her best, he was picking her up at 8pm, less than two hours away. She did not really know why she was so anxious to look good for that night. Part of her wanted to show him what he had been missing; part wanted him to want her again so that she could do the leaving this time and get her own back. But, whatever the reason, Nina was going to make a major effort. If she was to go out with him, she wanted to make sure she was looking gorgeous.

So, it was that she found herself half an hour later, lying up to her chin in bubbles, trying to get her mind on the following day and only thinking of Roberto. As she lay there, Nina could not help but be afraid of the days ahead. What if she fell for Roberto again? A familiar knot tightened in her stomach and she could feel her resolve clawing its way to the surface of her conscience. She had a job to do and she could not allow romance – any romance - to get in the way. She would see

Roberto tonight - for old time's sake - and that would be it. Then she could concentrate on finding Aelia's treasure. That was, after all, the real reason why she was here.

Indecision over what to wear is the plague of modern women and Nina was no exception. She was glad she had given herself plenty of time because she could not decide. Eventually, she opted for a pair of loose black linen slacks and a black halter neck top finished off with flat strappy sandals. Her long hair was clipped back into a loose chignon to show off the elegant curves of her neck and shoulders and she finished the ensemble off with pearl earrings her mother had given her and a silver bangle. She grabbed her only clutch bag and skipped downstairs.

Aunt Rosita was in the kitchen busy making traditional Mallorcan Festa fare for the tourists and locals that would drop into the café throughout the evening. "Nina, you look beautiful," Aunt Rosita said with pride. "Roberto is a lucky boy to be seen out with you tonight."

Nina shifted uncomfortably. "We're just going out as friends," she said looking down at her feet.

Rosita shrugged. "Good," she replied. "He doesn't deserve you."

She walked over and gave her niece a hug. Her eyes smiled. "Have a lovely time anyway," she whispered and kissed her on the cheek. "Remember – if he gives you trouble, I have plenty of knives!" Nina laughed.

"Nina! Roberto's here!" Jaume called from the café.

Her heart lodged itself in her throat and her stomach flipped.

"Coming!" she called back, the words tumbling out in a half squeak. She gave Rosita a quick kiss on the cheek. "I won't be late."

Standing at the bar talking to Javier, Roberto was looking devilishly handsome. A quick nod from Javier in Nina's direction caused Roberto to turn around quickly. His mouth dropped open in surprise.

He whistled his appreciation. "Nina! You look great."

"Thanks. So, do you," she replied automatically, then wished she hadn't. She still wanted him to suffer.

Looking at this tall man before her Nina was annoyed at still being impressed by his good looks. Roberto's crisp cream-coloured chinos and white short-sleeved designer shirt set off his honey-coloured tan. His short dark hair was shorn in a fashionable spikey style. He gave her a wolfish grin.

"Wait until Santos sees you," he said, "he'll never recognise you now you're a beautiful young woman."

She stood back. "Oh? What was I when he last saw me?"

"A young girl! I mean you were beautiful then too... it's just that now..."

She laughed and nudged him. "Relax. Some things don't change much, eh Roberto? You're still the same. And you scrub up not so badly yourself."

Roberto held out an arm.

"Is Cinderella ready to go to the ball?" he joked.

"I believe she is," Nina laughed slipping her arm into his. It felt reassuringly familiar and her heart skipped a beat. Steady, Nina, she scolded, steady. Breathing deeply to calm her nerves, Nina called goodbye to her family and arm in arm, she and Roberto walked out into the warm Spanish night. It felt good being with him again, like they had never been apart.

Nina was struck by how alive the town became at festival time. Everywhere she looked the narrow-cobbled streets were packed with tourists and locals. Under a canopy of twinkling lanterns music, laughter and shouts of 'Salute!' rang out as wine glasses were chinked in celebration of Alcudia's great saint, Sant Jaume. Roberto led Nina down a side-street that emerged onto the main road next to the old fortress gateway of Porta del Moll.

"This is a shortcut to Santos' bar. It's just down here." They passed a couple of small grocery shops, turned a corner into the modern part of town and came face-to-face with the gaudy pink neon of a bar proclaiming itself to be Santos'! Europop throbbed from within and the strong smell of hotdogs, chips and stale beer spilled out into the streets. Nina wrinkled her nose, but Roberto did not seem to notice.

"Here we are," he beamed. "Now what would you like to drink?"

"A beer would be great," Nina replied looking around for an empty table outside.

"Okay, you get the seats, I'll get the drinks."

He was soon lost in the tight throng of people drinking inside while Nina found a table and sat down. The street was crowded with smiling people going from bar to bar. Some wore garlands of flowers around their necks, other carried baskets of pastries they handed out to strangers. Nina smiled to herself as a young couple, tourists, probably German, stopped beside her and kissed. She wondered who they were and how they met. A voice snapped her back to the café.

"Jilted again?"

She turned around sharply. None other than Jay was standing at the table next to her. He pulled out a chair for an elegant dark-haired Spanish woman who nodded and smiled at Nina. She wore a sexy red strappy dress and elegant high-heels. Nina suddenly felt inadequate.

47

"No," Nina snapped. "He's gone to the bar to get some drinks. What brings you here anyway? I thought you said you were going to Palma?"

"I was and I did," he grinned, taking the seat directly behind her. "You'll like this: the meeting turned out to be a sham. The guy didn't have anything worth selling, so I split. Decided to swing by the north coast and look up the lovely Francesca."

He smiled over at his companion. She smiled back. Nina felt disgusted. They were like two love sick puppies, she thought.

"Jay, darling, aren't you going to introduce me to your friend?"

"I'm not his friend," Nina snapped. "I'd never be friends with a liar like him."

The woman flinched. She looked at Jay, obviously confused. Jay interjected.

"That's true," he said, "but I have manners and I'll introduce you anyway. Francesca Almovar, Nina Esposito," he said through gritted teeth.

Francesca nodded. "Hello," she said.

Nina returned the greeting and was about to turn away when Francesca asked "So how do you know darling Jay?"

God, does this woman never give up? She's going to be sorry she asked, thought Nina.

"To be perfectly honest, he stole something from me," she said.

Jay laughed. "I didn't steal it. It was there for the taking." He looked her straight in the eye. "You were just too slow."

"I had my seller all set up," she snapped. "You…." She fought for a word, "gazumped me." Her voice rose in anger.

"Gazumped? Now that's a great word. I didn't gazump you at all. You're just angry because I beat you to it."

Nina turned her back on him, arms folded tightly over her chest.

Jay leaned over and, ignoring her scowls, spoke softly. "I know a little secret about you Nina Esposito," he said.

"I have no secrets," she answered quickly. Nina shivered as his hot breath caressed her neck.

"Oh, I think you do." He shifted closer to her. "I know why you're really here and it's not for a holiday."

Nina felt the colour drain from her cheeks. She was grateful it was getting dark so he would not see.

"Oh really?" she said with an air of nonchalance. "If I'm not here on holiday, why am I here?" There was no way he could know.

"I believe you're here over the matter of some treasure," he said, grinning from ear to ear. "Am I right?"

Nina's dark eyes flashed in anger. How did he...? She wouldn't let him know he had rattled her.

She composed herself. "I don't know what you mean," she said airily. "What treasure? I'm here to visit family and take a well-earned break. Not that it's any of your business."

"Ah, but it is if there's booty to be had," he said. "Want to hear my theory on the real reason you are here?"

She shook her head.

He continued anyway: "I reckon you're here to search for something special. Considering this is Alcudia, I would hazard the guess that you're here to find a certain infamous and mythical necklace. Am I right?"

"No, you're not right," she hissed. "I'm here to visit my aunt and uncle. I've not visited them for years. I fancied a break, so I came here. Okay?"

"Then why did my source tell me differently?" he asked.

"What source?"

He tapped the end of his nose and said nothing more, merely sat back in his chair and smiled. Nina threw him a dirty look and turned her back on him again. She hated him with a passion and wished he would go away. Where was Roberto? He had been away for ages. Surely it did not take this long to get two glasses of Cerveza in? Then an idea entered her head.

Turning to Francesca, she said: "So, are you two going anywhere to celebrate the festa tonight? If you are, you'd better hurry or you'll miss the procession through the Old Town. It's the best bit."

And then I will get rid of you both and relax and enjoy the rest of the evening, she thought.

"Jay's taking me to a concert in Palma," Francesca smiled. "I'm really looking forward to it. He's been promising me he'd take me for years."

"Sounds like him." Nina turned on Jay. "He's the type of man who is always making promises…and then lets you down."

"Now hold on a minute!" Jay protested. "I never promised you anything…!"

"There's no use denying it, Jay," Nina said triumphantly. "You're just a cad who uses seduction as a way of stealing from other people."

He glared at her. "I can see there's no use talking to you in this mood," he said quietly. "Perhaps Francesca and I should go and leave you to it."

"Perhaps you should," she snapped.

Lips pursed, she pretended to be fascinated by a group of tourists who were dancing past in a long snake of limbo dancers. She watched them, telling herself that Jay was not really there. She tapped her nails on the table, impatient for rescue by Roberto, but still he did not return. She sensed Jay and the woman rising from their table and make ready to go. "I think you've been abandoned again," smirked Jay.

"Are you still here?" Nina growled. "Roberto's obviously been held up at the bar. That's all. He'll be here in a minute." She strained to see him. "In fact, here he is." Relief washed over her as the handsome Spaniard emerged from the crowded bar holding two large glasses of foaming beer. He smiled as he caught sight of Nina. She waved back.

"It was really busy in there," he laughed. Seeing Jay and Francesca, he said: "Hello? Are you friends of Nina."

"Apparently not," Jay answered smoothly, throwing Nina a look. "C'mon, Francesca, we've got a concert to attend. The atmosphere here's got decidedly chilly."

Francesca gave Nina a stern look before taking Jay's arm. As they squeezed past Nina Jay made sure he gave her a rough shove. "What was that all about?" Roberto asked plonking himself down beside Nina.

She sighed. "That was Jay Reynolds," she replied, "but forget about him. He's nobody. Let's just enjoy our drinks."

She took a sip of beer and tried to relax. Jay might think he knew all about her plans, but he did not know she had Harper's transcript and the priest's text. Or did he? He had found out about her coming to Mallorca. Who could have told him? If he knew the real reason she was here, how much more did he know? Maybe he had information that she didn't! Maybe he was going to look for the necklace himself. She could not let him snatch any treasure from under her nose again. She felt sick. She took a nervous swig of her beer and sat the glass on the table.

"Roberto," she said, suddenly anxious to leave. "I hope you

don't mind. I'm feeling a bit tired. I think I might go back to my aunt's house. I've got an early start tomorrow."

His eyes twinkled as he smiled.

"Going treasure hunting again?" he asked slowly.

Was there anyone on this island who did not know her business?

"What do you mean?" She fought to keep the annoyance out of her voice.

"It's your job isn't it? Your passion," he answered, dark eyes twinkling. "Nina, honey, I know you. I'm guessing you're going looking for something again. You were always searching for – what was it? A necklace? – when you were here before, so why should you be any different now? You can't help yourself. Am I right?"

She shrugged. "You really do know me. Always was on the lookout for something…"

"Maybe I can help you."

She was unsure. Could she trust him?

"Okay, you got me. I had thought I might have another look for Aelia's tomb and her necklace while I was here." She did a hands-up. "What can I say? I'm an archaeologist. I can't help myself."

"Do you need a companion?"

He leaned across the table. He smelled great, he looked great. She felt a sudden wave of desire wash over her. God, he's still as sexy, she thought. She felt her resolve to keep him at arm's length weaken. And maybe she could do with some help….

"No, thank you," she heard herself saying.

"Oh, are you sure?" he replied, disappointed.

"Absolutely. Now, if you don't mind, Roberto. I really would like to go home."

"But, what about the Festa? Santos was really looking forward to seeing you."

She thought for a minute. "Well maybe I could stay for a little while longer."

Chapter 4

NINA got up early the next morning with a pounding headache and the guilt you get following a drunken night where memories are patchy at best. She felt uncomfortable about something but did not know what. She had gone out with the intention of not overindulging, but her plans were soon scuppered by an eager Roberto and the equally enthusiastic Santos who insisted on keeping the beer flowing for his brother and his companion.

Memories of last night were coming back in flashbacks; there had been dancing and more drinking and…oh God…did she really sing karaoke? She groaned and hid her head in her hands. What else had happened? She looked around her room. There was no sign of anyone else having been there. She lifted the bed clothes and was relieved to find herself fully dressed bar her shoes which she supposed must be on the floor somewhere. So, she concluded, I spent the night in my own bed, fully clothed, and alone. Thank God. She sighed with relief as she recalled Roberto walking her back to her aunt's and trying to kiss her on the doorstep. She had sidestepped his advances, shoving him back out into the square with a giggle. Then everything was a blank…she must have somehow got herself upstairs to bed. She could not remember. She shuddered with shame and embarrassment and hoped none of her family had witnessed her drunken return.

"What time is it?" she muttered to herself, reaching over to the dressing table and scrambling about for her mobile phone.

It was six o'clock, time to get up. She sat up and groaned as a thousand tiny mallets whacked against her skull. She was never drinking beer again. A wave of nausea swept over her and she quickly lay down again until it had passed. She was never, never drinking again!

An hour later than planned, Nina rose, showered and got dressed. Eyes heavy with lack of sleep and too much alcohol, she slunk into the kitchen and sat down at the big wooden table, fragile and mentally punishing herself for over indulging. There was no-one about, but her Aunt Rosa must have already got up because there was a pot of fresh coffee gurgling on the stove. Nina shuffled over and poured herself a mug. She shut her eyes and waited until the latest lurch of nausea passed.

"Never, never again," she resolved.

She took sip of coffee and, hoping it would restore her equilibrium. She couldn't let a hangover hold her back any more than it had already. She fetched Harper's diary from her rucksack and opened the battered covers. As she poured over the pages in the soft early morning sunlight, her cousin Jaume appeared at the door.

"Your boyfriend's here," he said before disappearing again.

She did not have much time to react before Roberto's smiling face popped around the door. Nina barely managed a weak smile. She was not expecting him this morning. She might have made arrangements with him to meet up again that night, but she was already having second thoughts about that. He looked surprisingly fresh despite keeping up with her drink for drink and not leaving her until after one.

"Good, you are up. Now, when are we getting started? Are you ready now?" He came in and sat down beside her.

"Roberto, I said I didn't need help," she said cautiously.

"I know, but you always say that. And I thought it might be fun," he said, white teeth showing through a wide smile. "Besides, I really enjoyed being with you last night."

She didn't reply. With the woolly-headedness of the hangover and the shock of his insisting on helping, she could not think of anything polite to say to get rid of him. The best she could muster was a pained smile, which was enough for him to reach across the table and take her hand. It was all she could do to stop herself instinctively pulling it away.

"Let me help," he said gently pleading.

She shook her head. "I don't need any complications."

"There won't be any, I promise!"

"I don't know," she found her voice. "I'm used to working on my own. I don't really like having anyone else there."

He looked downhearted. "I won't interfere. I won't speak. You won't even know I'm there."

"I'm sorry."

"Okay, I respect your decision. I know when I'm beat. I will let you get on with your adventure. Without me. Maybe I'll see you later?" he added hopefully.

She said nothing, nodded and watched as he stood up and walked head down to the door. He looked like a puppy that had just been kicked. Something melted inside her.

"Well, goodbye then," he said, lips tight with disappointment.

"Bye," she said wanting to stop him, but unable to.

His head reappeared at the doorway seconds later.

"Are you really sure you don't want some help? Two heads are better than one? Isn't that what you British say? I could carry the lunches!" he asked, eyes bright with hope.

"Oh, all right!" she cried. "You can come with me! Just don't get in my way!"

"Great! You won't regret this," he replied, the wide grin back on his face. I hope not, thought Nina as she inhaled the citrus scent of his aftershave. He smelled great. Oh God, this was going to be difficult.

"Now what's first, boss?" he joked jerking her back to the present. "Is there anything I can do? Are we ready to go treasure hunting?"

"Not quite." She nodded towards the stove. "Help yourself to coffee and come have a look at this."

"What is it?"

"I want to go over this notebook again. There are pages missing from it, but hopefully you and I can work out what those missing clues might be."

"Let me see," he said, peering over her shoulder at the battered notebook in front of her.

"If I'm right, this could lead me to Aelia's necklace," she said.

Nina explained about Joseph Harper's lifelong search. She told him how she had got his notebook but felt it best to leave out the bit about the priest's text. She wasn't sure how much she should tell him. Could she trust him? She didn't know, but as she was starting to feel glad he was there she threw caution to the wind.

"I've gone through the notebook and basically it talks about how Dr Harper had first come to hear about the legend and his thoughts on the authenticity of the story. It seems he and his wife had first come to Mallorca in the '70s on holiday. They had friends here; the eminent Spanish historian Manuel Astray, who had befriended Harper years before when Astray and his wife had left Spain, fleeing Franco. Anyway, it was Astray who told Harper about the story. Following the death of Franco, Harper came to Mallorca to look into the legend and, according to this book, he found clues to its possible whereabouts in references to it within the Sant Jaume Church and the Victoria Hermitage," she traced the words on the page with her finger. "Some of the stonework used to build both came from earlier times, Roman times, and he claims some of the largest stones still have faint carvings depicting Aelia's burial."

"So, what happened? Why didn't Harper find the necklace?" Roberto wanted to know.

"I don't know. The missing pages might have explained it. I wonder who would have done such a thing and why?" she pondered. "No matter, there are plenty of clues still left. We just have to work them out."

She closed the notebook and looked at him.

"Well?" she said, standing up and pushing the chair back. She stuffed the diary into her rucksack. "Are you coming to help me look?"

He got to his feet quickly and smiled.

"Try and stop me," he said.

Nina wanted to start at the Church of St Jaume in the centre of the old town. It lay within the medieval walls, and was built in the 19th century to replace the original 14th century church after it collapsed, leaving the baroque Sant Crist Chapel and altarpiece the only things still standing. As it was only a few yards from the ruins of the old Roman city, Harper suspected the Alcudians had used Roman stones when rebuilding it.

It was only ten minutes from the café and despite it being early, Nina and Roberto were hot and perspiring when they arrived at the small square in front of the church. She had forgotten just how warm it got in Mallorca and was glad of the comforting darkness once inside. As her eyes adjusted to the dimness, she could see the simple layout.

"What are we doing here?" whispered Roberto crossing himself.

Nina smiled. She had forgotten churches made him uncomfortable.

"Waiting for you to give me an aria," she smirked.

He scowled. "I wish I had never told you about that. It's been a long time since I've been to church let alone been an altar boy."

"And you a good Catholic boy as well. What happened? Fallen out with God?"

Roberto made a face.

"Don't worry," she continued. "I'll never speak of it again." She giggled. "C'mon. I need to have a look at the fonda. According to Harper's notes, there's an interesting inscription on the base of the statue of Saint Andre."

They made their way through a stone archway to the chapel of Sant Andre. It was situated off the main building, in a secluded spot at the sunniest side of the church. Nina sighed with relief when she saw it was empty. That meant she could go about her investigation unhindered. It took them only a few minutes to find the statue, so she instructed Roberto to keep a watch out for priests as she stepped over a rope barrier that held the public back from the ancient effigy. Beautifully carved out of a single piece of rock and standing against a wall, the Sant Andre statue stared imperiously over her head. According to tradition it cried tears of real blood in August 1508, sparking centuries of worship and devotion.

Nina crouched down to have a look at the base. Although the chapel was well lit, she couldn't quite make out the markings so turned on the torch app on her phone. It cast a small beam of light on the base, placed hard up against the wall.

"Do you see anything yet?" Roberto called from the doorway.

Her voice was muffled. "No, there doesn't seem to be anything… Oh, hold on a minute. What's this?" Nina angled her phone and took a few snaps. The flash bounced sparks of light off the walls.

"Someone's coming!" Roberto whispered urgently, prompting Nina to stuff her phone into her pocket, scramble to her feet and rush to sit with Roberto on one of the pews. Quickly, they took up pious positions, hands clasped in prayer, eyes raised to heaven, pretending to be deep in contemplation. Footsteps echoed up to the entranceway and a young priest's head popped round the doorway.

"Oh, I'm sorry," he exclaimed, startled to see them. "I didn't know anyone had come in. I beg your pardon for interrupting your prayers. I will leave you. Excuse me."

Obviously embarrassed, he disappeared back the way he had come. They waited until his footsteps had died before expelling sighs of relief. How could they have ever explained to him what they were doing here? Nina looked at Roberto. Roberto looked at Nina. They burst out laughing.

"Did you see his face?" wheezed Roberto.

"I know, I thought he was going to die!" she giggled. She got to her feet. "Right, come on," she said. "I think I've got everything I need here."

"What did you find?" he asked.

"I'll tell you outside."

In the courtyard, shading their eyes against the sharp Mallorcan light, Nina told Roberto what she had discovered.

"There was a piece of writing in Latin. I couldn't quite make it out, but I definitely saw the name Livius and what looked like a carving depicting a burial. I need to get these photos downloaded on to my laptop, so I can study them better."

"Doesn't Harper's book tell you all this?"

"Yes, but I need to start from the beginning. I have to gather all the Roman clues together and look at them objectively. Maybe then I can see something that Harper missed."

There was a pause as Roberto looked back at the church thoughtfully.

"You want all the Roman things together?"

"That's right."

"And do you know where they might be?"

"In the ground?"

"Or… in a museum!" He pointed to an arched wooden doorway.

"Nina, you do know this church has one of its own now, don't you?" She nodded. "Lead the way!"

The golden bronze bust of a beautiful young girl gazed out from behind its glass casing. Her hair was worn high, fancy earrings adorned her ears. She wore a stola, the traditional attire of a Roman noblewoman, and around her neck, in all its golden glory, was a fabulous necklace. Nina gasped when she saw it. Below the casing, was a plaque: Roman circa 130AD. Nina looked for Roberto. She had left him happily chatting to a friend at the door of the museum and she had come in alone. He would have to see this. Surely this girl was Aelia? It couldn't be anyone else.

"Are you thinking what I'm thinking?"

Nina spun around.

Jay Reynolds was smirking back at her.

She frowned and turned away from him. Maybe if she didn't look at him, he would disappear. He would not ruin this moment for her.

"You can turn your back on me if you want, but it won't change the fact that this is not Livius' daughter, Aelia."

He strode around the bust and peered through the glass at Nina, a smile playing about his lips.

"If it's not her, then who is it?" Nina couldn't stop herself from saying. Damn it. Why did she always fall into his trap? He was goading her, she knew that. He wanted to engage her in conversation so he could mock her and show her how clever he was. She would not give him the satisfaction.

He walked around and stood beside her. Without taking his gaze off the beautiful girl statue, he said: "It's Venus. It was found near her temple in Pollentia. However, if you haven't done your homework properly, you wouldn't know that."

"What makes you think I haven't?"

"Oh c'mon, it's me you're talking to. You're so obsessed with Aelia you're hardly thinking straight."

"I don't know what you mean," she said quickly, unable to meet his gaze.

"Sure, you don't."

He stepped away from her and moved towards the door.

He turned around.

"You know, if you ever need my help, you've only got to ask. We could find that necklace together."

"Who says I'm looking for the necklace? I told you before, I'm here on holiday." She was defiant.

"Nina, lovely Nina. I'm not stupid. I heard about the discovery of the priest's text. I knew the British Museum would send their best to look for it." He studied her for a reaction, adding: "Let me help. Think about it. We'd make a great team."

She could feel her blood boiling. Don't let him get to you, she told herself. Don't rise to him.

"No, I don't think so," she snapped.

"Why not?" He seemed genuinely surprised.

"My perfume bottle is why not," she said.

"That again? I told you before I didn't know that's what you were after. It's not my fault I got there before you. Are you going to let a petty thing like that come between us?"

"There is no 'us'! And we would not make a great team!" she growled. "I wouldn't work with you if you were the last archaeologist on Earth."

"That's a bit harsh."

"Good. That's how I meant it."

He held up his hands. "Okay, I get the hint." He turned to leave. "But, if you ever need help, you've just got to ask."

Jay pulled open the door and was about to walk out when Nina's fury burst out of her.

"You are the most infuriating, the most horrible man I've ever met," she shouted after him through gritted teeth. He turned and looked at her. "And if I ever needed your help, which I don't, I would rather bite off my right arm and run down the street, swinging it and singing the Halleluiah Chorus than ask you for it."

He laughed.

"Well put," he said.

Smiling, he strolled towards her, eyes never leaving hers. She stood her ground. She was not afraid of him, although the wobble in her knees would beg to differ. He was just so handsome. Stop it! Stop it!

"You know," he said. "I love it when a woman gets angry. It brings out a certain sparkle in her eyes, a flush in her cheek." He was nearly on her. "It's quite...sexy."

He was now standing very close to her, almost touching. The heat from his body and the intensity of his gaze was making her feel uncomfortably weak, but she couldn't draw herself away. Her stomach did back flips and her mouth was dry. His blue eyes twinkled, amused. He knew the effect he was having on her.

"Get away from me," her voice was hoarse, cracked. She took a step back.

"Why? Is the great Nina Esposito feeling nervous? Around me?" His voice was low, dangerously husky.

She took another step away, but there was no escape. She was backed up right against the glass case containing the golden girl; trapped. Jay was not about to let her escape. His breathing became shallower as he pressed his body hard against hers. She put her hands up to his chest to hold him back and a thrill went through her as she felt the toned muscles beneath his shirt. She could not take her eyes away from his, or object, as she felt his hands slip around her waist and pull her towards him. She felt helpless and scared and excited all at once. Gently, slowly, he moved in towards her for a kiss and she found herself responding. His lips were soft as they brushed against hers and a small gasp of pleasure escaped from her as he moved to nuzzle her ear.

"Still nervous, Nina?" he whispered.

"I...don't...know," she murmured eliciting a chuckle from him.

He pulled back and surveyed her triumphantly.

"You can't resist me, can you?" he smirked. "I knew there was still something there."

Nina snapped back to reality and glared at him. "That meant nothing!" she growled, suddenly finding her voice and furious with him, with herself, for letting her guard down. "You mean nothing. Get off me!" she snapped pushing him away.

"Fine," he said releasing her and standing back. "But you know where I am."

"I'll never need you," said Nina curtly.

"We really would make a great team, Nina," he added.

"No, we wouldn't Jay. Teams are made of people who trust each other. You're a lying thief and I don't trust you!"

"But you trust your Spanish boyfriend?"

"He's not my boyfriend," she hissed.

"Glad to hear it," Jay replied, blue eyes sparkling.

With that parting shot, he strode confidently out of the room without looking back leaving the stricken Nina stunned and unable to move. Her thoughts were bouncing around her head, jumbled and indecipherable. She couldn't believe Jay Reynolds had just kissed her and left, and yet couldn't move to do anything about it. She felt weak and sick. What strange power does he have over me to leave me in such a mess? She wondered. He's handsome but insufferable, my least favourite kind of man. She steadied herself, trying to make sense of what had happened and cursing her own body for responding so quickly to Jay's advances. It was in this nervous state that Roberto found her.

"Nina? Are you all right? I just saw Jay Reynolds outside. He said you weren't feeling well." He went to put his arm around her, but she shrugged him off. She didn't need another man getting fresh with her today.

"I'm fine," she said, managing a smile. "Just a bit lightheaded that's all…must have been the sight of that odious man."

"Jay?"

"Yes, I can't stand him," she said not sure who she was trying to convince, Roberto or herself. "He's horrible," she added staring at the door. Then she turned to look at Roberto, eyes imploring. "And worse than that, he knows why I'm here. I don't know how, but he knows. I need to get to the necklace before Jay Reynolds does. I can't let him find it first, I can't."

"I will do everything I can to help." He took her hand and looked deeply into her eyes. "I would do anything for you. You know that."

Except stay with me when we were younger, she thought.

"That's a dangerous promise," she said.

Joseph Harper's Diary - 9th September, 1979

Persuaded Mary to let me travel up to the spring close to the Victoria Hermitage. She said she and Jack would do their own thing. She's not talking to me. Says I'm obsessed with finding this dead body. I told her I was doing it in the interests of history. She didn't reply, merely dragged Jack away. Don't know where they went to. She never said when they returned later.

The Hermitage is quite stunning, but I couldn't find the spring at first. One of the priests told me it had dried up years ago. I said I wanted to go looking for it anyway. He pointed me in the right direction and I began to climb. I nearly missed it, it was so tiny, but I found my spring. A little trickle of water dribbling down the mountainside. No sign of Aelia's tomb.

This mystery is perplexing. Wonder if I'll ever find her?

Following her run-in with Jay Reynolds, Nina was reluctant to share her thoughts about the gold statue with Roberto for fear of him thinking her stupid. Instead, she purchased a postcard of it and tucked it into her bag for studying later. She took a quick look around the rest of the museum's artifacts to make sure they hadn't missed anything. Apart from a few pieces of broken pottery and war memorabilia, there wasn't much else that could lead her to the necklace. She left feeling slightly disappointed. She had hoped there would have been something…

"Where to now, boss?" Roberto joked.

"The Victoria Hermitage. Harper's journal says there's an ancient Roman spring nearby where they've found coins dating back to the Emperor Augustus. Harper seemed to think it is the same 'spring of life' that only runs every few years, where Aelia would meet her lover. There are no other streams in this area, so he went there and that's where we're going now."

"You want us to walk there?" Roberto seemed stunned at the prospect. The spring was some 7km from the town centre and 200 metres above sea level.

"No," Nina replied. "I wondered if we might borrow Uncle Javier's car and drive there. We could park off the main road and walk from there. It's a lovely day and a stroll in the hills might do us good."

"In this heat?" Roberto asked incredulously.

She nodded.

"If you say so."

Chapter 5

JAVIER did not mind lending his niece his precious car; he knew she would take care of it. He did not ask where Nina and Roberto were going; he presumed they were going to the beach and Nina did not offer any information to the contrary. She loved her aunt and uncle but could not be bothered going through the whys and wherefores of her search. Like most people on this island, they thought the legend was just that – a legend and nothing more. They would never understand why it meant so much to Nina.

The Hermitage was within a half hour's drive from Alcudia, along a winding, well-kept road. Built by Pere Torrandell in 1679 on a peak overlooking the town to the west and the rugged coast to the north the sanctuary was dedicated to Our Lady de la Victoria. Her fine 15th century statue stood proudly at the high altar. But it wasn't the statue Nina was after, it was clues.

"What are we doing here?" Roberto asked as Nina got out the car. "I need to find that spring. If I can find it, maybe I can figure out where Aelia's family hid her body," she replied, nose in Harper's notebook.

"Great. But do you think we can stop for some lunch first?"

he said patting his stomach. "I'm really hungry."

She smiled. "I don't see why not. Can we get lunch here?"

"That's not possible." They spun round to see a short, balding man in priest's garb. "This is a place of retreat. If you have come to pray, you will be most welcome. However, if you have come to eat there is a small café a short walk from here. You can get lunch there."

"Thank you, Father," Nina said. "We're most grateful." Then she paused. Maybe he could help them. "We've not come to pray, Father. We're looking for something. I wonder if you can help us?"

"I will do my best," the priest smiled.

"There should be small spring nearby. Possibly dating from Roman times. Do you know of it? Have you seen it or heard stories about it?"

His hand went to his chin as he thought. "No, there are no streams around here. Definitely not."

Nina closed her eyes.

"Unless you count the one about a kilometre north-east of here, in the mountainside?" he said. "They say it only appears when the rains are heavy every few years. Could that be it?"

Nina felt a tremor of excitement pass through her body. "I hope so," she replied, eyes shining. "Thank you, Father, you've been a great help."

Nodding, the priest thanked her and bade her a good journey.

She turned to Roberto. "Are you up for a hike?"

"Yes. Right after we get some food. I'm starving!" he pleaded. He looked so forlorn that Nina gave in. She supposed she could wait a half hour longer.

They left the car and took the dusty road towards a small

white villa in the distance. It was hot work under the midday sun and they were relieved when the road turned to reveal the villa was in fact the café the priest had mentioned. Under the shade of the battered yellow awning, they chose two white plastic chairs that gave them a view of the valley below. An unsmiling girl appeared and thrust a couple of laminated menus at them, in English with pictures of everything on offer.

"I see the waitresses have lost none of their charm," Nina giggled as the she disappeared inside.

Roberto feigned mock indignation. "Hey, I used to be a waiter," he said, "and a damned good one at that."

"How could I ever forget?" she replied smiling.

As they took in the view, Nina wondered whether Aelia and her lover had seen the same view all those centuries ago, whether they really had visited the spring. Before she realised he had even gone Roberto was coming back carrying two ice cold beers.

"I come bearing gifts," he said as he plonked a frothy glass in front of her. "I hope you don't mind but I've ordered us a toastie each. I know how much you used to like them."

"That's fine," she replied and relaxed into her chair, beer glass in hand. Closing her eyes, she raised the beer to her lips and took a sip, listening to the crickets in the bushes as the cold, reviving liquid went down. Sitting there in a mountain café with her former lover she felt she might never want to leave. Neither of them said anything.

Then: "Do you think we'll find the spring?" she said after a time.

"It could be having one of its dry spells," Roberto replied.

"I know, I've thought of that." She looked back up the mountain. "I hope not."

"Two toasted sandwiches." The waitress was back bearing their order. The heavenly aroma made Nina's stomach grumble and her mouth water. She hadn't realised she was so hungry. They tucked in, with Nina wolfing down lunch like there was no tomorrow.

"I see you haven't lost any of your appetite in the last ten years," joked Roberto. His dark eyes smiling.

"Well, I'm a growing girl," she replied with mock indignation.

"So I see!" he said patting her flat stomach.

"Hey! Don't be so cheeky!"

They were interrupted by the sight of a large black car weaving its way up the road. It was a huge American sedan of the type used by diplomats that looked totally out of place on this narrow mountain roadway. The windows were blacked out but the private plates bore the name: Santana 10.

Nina shielded her eyes from the sun's glare to get a better look. "I haven't seen one of those for years."

"It's a beauty," Roberto agreed. He was studying it. "Just a minute," he said.

"What?"

"I think I know that car." He leapt up excitedly. "Yes, I'm sure I know that car."

"Well, there can't be many others like it here."

The car drew up to the café and the driver, wearing smart trousers and a short-sleeved white shirt and blue tie, got out. He opened a rear passenger door and Nina and Roberto heard a man's voice giving the driver instructions about the type of canned drink he wanted. A wide grin spread across Roberto's face. He got up and ran over to the car.

He knocked on one of the blacked-out windows shouting: "Hallo! It's me! Roberto. Roberto Mendieta!"

The window slid down and Nina saw the profile of an older man. He seemed pleased to see Roberto and chatted animatedly to her friend for a few minutes, but she couldn't make out what he was saying. She watched the two men converse. Then, when the driver returned, the conversation ended and the window slid back up. Roberto returned to her beaming.

"You'll never guess who that was," he said. And without waiting for her reply, he continued: "Only the top man on the island. Only Costa Santana."

"Who?" Was she supposed to know who this man was?

"A local businessman, a millionaire. Billionaire even." Roberto watched as the car slid out of view. "And – he's a very good friend of my father. He said he'd like to meet you."

"Really? Then why didn't he wait?"

"He was in a hurry. He apologised for having to leave, but…. and this is great…he's invited us to his yacht for dinner tomorrow night." Roberto hardly seemed able to contain his excitement.

"Wait until you see this yacht, it's so impressive!" he gushed. "It's got a cinema room, a huge boardroom and its own swimming pool. There's a helipad and…"

Nina let Roberto ramble on, lost in her own thoughts. That will be another evening lost, she thought. Then again, she could see how much he wanted this and being absolutely truthful, she was more than a bit curious. After all, how often do you get the chance to find out what a millionaire's yacht looked like?

"Roberto, over there!" Nina called as she scrambled over rocks towards a clump of dry grasses.

Her sharp hearing had picked up the faint sound of a trickle from somewhere in the dense undergrowth. She stopped in her tracks and listened. Yes, there it was again, the unmistakeable sound of water. At last there it was, close to the peak of the hill, a thin ribbon of water meandering down through the undergrowth to the sea. Nina smiled triumphantly as Roberto joined her.

"I knew you would find it," he said softly.

Surrounded by rocks and shrubbery there was nothing to suggest anyone had visited the spring for a long time, let alone the Romans. Nina searched desperately for a clue, a sign of ruins or earthworks, but found none. She sat on a rock and stared at the water, willing a piece of irrefutable evidence to show itself. When nothing did, she had to admit it: Harper was right, there was nothing here.

She took her camera from her backpack and took a couple of shots anyway...you never knew, something might show up in the photographs. Nina signed to Roberto that she was ready to go. It was too hot out here anyway. She took one last glance at the water and then left, puzzled at the spring's significance… if this was indeed the spring. Taking Roberto's hand, allowing him to assist her down the mountainside, Nina's mind was awash with possibilities. Maybe there was more here in Aelia's time. Maybe she should come back and dig nearby. Maybe, maybe, maybe. She sighed. Maybe she would work it out later.

Chapter 6

JOSEPH Harper's Diary - 5th September, 1979
After I had seen Juan Sebastian, I decided to go scouting for some clues. I chose a local tavern and asked mine host what he thought of the Aelia legend. The man, a convivial chap, said it was all a children's story and not to believe the fairytales that some people spread. However, if I really wanted to know more about it, he said, I should seek out Anna Maria Martinez, a widow of the village. She was the local storyteller, he said, her family had held the honour of the title for centuries, and she would know more than anyone about it all. I asked him where she lived. He told me. So, I drained my beer, the excellent local stuff, and left.

Senora Martinez was at first reticent about talking to me about Aelia. She accused me of seeking her out to laugh at her. Madam, I assured her, nothing could be further from my thoughts. Eventually, I persuaded her that my intentions were honourable and she invited me into her modest little house. We talked for more than an hour. Senora Martinez told me everything she knew about the Roman noblewoman. Aelia was reputed to have been a beauty in her day and her love affair with Marcus Scaveola was one of the greatest love stories of all times, she said.

"What of her tomb?" I asked her. "Where was she buried?"

Senora Martinez said it was a secret, nobody knew. She could only say that it was thought to lie between three places Aelia loved most. I asked her was those were and she said she didn't know. She told me, however, that Aelia and Marcus were supposed to have met secretly at a spring in the mountains, and that Aelia was said to have worshipped in a cave now known as the Sant Marti Cave.

"And the third?" I asked her excitedly.

"Ahh. Now, that's the real mystery of her story..." she smiled.

Nina gazed at the map spread out on her bed. She traced the route she and Roberto took earlier from the Sant Jaume Church to the Hermitage. There had been barely a trickle of water at the site of the spring, let alone any signs of two tragic Roman lovers. She flicked through Harper's diary, picking up where she had left off. She read: According to local legend, Aelia's family buried her body in a most sacred place, surrounded by orange trees and beautiful flowers. They chose a spot within a few miles of Pollentia, a spot in the centre of the places Aelia loved the most so that, from her resting place, her spirit might rise from the ground and take pleasure in them as she had done in life.

Nina marked the spring on the map with a black marker pen. Then she drew a star over the Sant Marti Caves. Where else might a young Roman woman like to go? She circled the theatre and drew a question mark. The baths? Another circle. Lightly, she joined them. It formed a square over several miles of countryside. The centre was in the middle of nowhere, in what looked like a field. Surely, they wouldn't have buried her there? It was too far away from anything that Aelia might have liked, so how could she have seen any of these places from her last resting place? Nina studied the photographs she'd taken earlier of the markings on the statue and of the spring. The markings looked like long thin scratches in the stonework. They were indecipherable as words, if, indeed, they had ever been words in the first place. The spring looked like a hole in the ground sprouting water. There were no further clues in Harper's diary. She was well and truly stumped. There was only one thing she could think of doing and that was to go to the San Marti Caves, then to the place on the map she believed was the centre of Aelia's favourite places and investigate. She looked at her watch: 9pm, too late to go hunting tonight, yet too early to go to bed and Aelia could wait until tomorrow. She decided to go downstairs and have a drink in the bar. A glass of wine would hit the spot and, besides, Rosita and Javier would be there to talk to. She was sure there was still a lot of family news still to be caught up on. She stood up and looked at herself in the mirror. Her face was a little pink from the sun and her hair ruffled. She applied some lipstick. Her lips tingled as she remembered the kiss in the museum and cursed Jay Reynolds for getting her so hot and bothered. She hadn't enjoyed it one bit, had she?

"Most definitely not!" she said out loud as if trying to convince herself. Dismissing Jay from her thoughts, Nina pulled on a fine wool cardigan and left her bedroom. She could return to the puzzle of Aelia's treasure and Jay Reynold's insult tomorrow.

The café was as busy as it had always been. Light, airy and full of happy people enjoying the ambience and generosity of Mallorcan hospitality. Behind the bar, Javier was his usual jolly self, laughing heartily at his friends' jokes. His wife was busy chatting to tourists as she collected glasses from the tables outside. The television, showing athletics highlights, was blaring above the tables in the corner. Nina smiled to herself. Nothing changes, she thought.

Javier greeted her. "Nina, my dear, come and join us. I'd like you to meet some people."

Automatically, he reached for a wine glass and poured her his favourite red. Plonking it in front of her, he introduced his friends one by one. Pedro, the shy one; Michael, the fat town councillor; Jaun, the joker. Nina greeted them all with a smile and a nod of the head.

"And you know Dr Reynolds," Javier finished. Nina's stomach flipped. She hadn't seen Jay sitting behind the bulk of Michael. Damn it! What's he doing here?

"Nina," Jay said. And then, as if reading her thoughts: "I came by take your aunt and uncle up on their offer of hospitality."

"Oh, I'm sorry Uncle Javier didn't call me earlier," she said with more than a hint of sarcasm. "It's late and you must be about to leave."

"Oh no," he said, smiling. "I've just arrived. Luckily, Javier had a spare room to rent. Looks like we'll be roommates," he chuckled.

"What?"

"We'll be under the same roof," he grinned. "Looks like my room is near yours."

"I don't think that's such a good idea," she blurted out.

Javier frowned at her.

"Why not? He's a paying guest," he said incredulously. "Besides any friend of Nina's is a friend of ours!"

"I mean... Oh, I don't know what I mean," she sighed grabbing her glass of wine. "Anyway, I only came to get this." She waggled the glass at her uncle. "I'm going to bed Uncle Javier. It's been a long day and I'm tired. Good night."

"See you tomorrow," her uncle replied.

She said her goodbyes and shot Jay a scowl before turning heel and marching through the back. She may have to be under the same roof as him, but she did not have to be in the same bar. Tiredness overcame her with every step up to her room. Her feet and her eyes battled it out for which felt the heaviest. She had only bidden Roberto farewell a few hours before and had spent the entire evening holed up in her room going over what little clues there were. She was exhausted. It had indeed been a long day.

She did not hear the footsteps coming up the marble tiled steps behind her.

"Nina?" It was Jay.

She turned at the top of the stairs.

"What do you want?" she growled. "Have you come to force yourself on me again?"

In the dimly light, Nina could barely make out the features of his face. He seemed bemused.

"I thought the attraction was mutual," he said. His voice was low and husky, his eyes liquid with desire for her. "I'm sorry if I offended you."

"So you should be," she snapped.

"Look, I don't know what's got into you, Nina. We used to be more than good friends...don't you remember?"

"Friends don't steal from friends," she hissed and turned to go. He grabbed her arm and spun her around to face him again.

"Okay, so I got the bottle. Big deal. It's done and I'm sorry I upset you. Can we start again? I'd like us to be friends," he let go of her arm and offered her his hand. She looked at it disdainfully, then turned away.

"I don't think so, Jay," she said as she reached for the door to her room and opened it. "Good night."

Behind her she could hear him hesitate on the landing. He let out a sigh and seemed to decide to return to the bar, but stopped halfway down the stairs. She heard his footsteps come back up and stop outside her door. She turned to face him as he entered her room.

"You know something? You are one pain in the ass, Nina Esposito," he said, eyes blazing with anger.

"It takes one to know one!" she retorted.

They glared at each other for a few seconds.

"Get out of my room!" she yelled.

"Fine I will," he replied, "but not before I tell you a few home truths. I came to Alcudia to try and make peace with you. I know what I did was wrong, particularly as we had been getting so close, and I just wanted to say that I'm sorry."

"About time! You've said it, now go away!" she snapped.

"Not before I do this!"

Before she could stop him, he strode across her room, gathered her in his arms and was kissing her passionately on the lips. She struggled to free herself from his strong grip, but the feel of his warm body hard against hers and his heavenly smell made her giddy. She stopped resisting and kissed him back. Before she knew it, they were on the bed.

"What about Francesca?" she asked between hot kisses.

"What about her?"

"Won't she be upset that her boyfriend is making love to another woman?"

"I suppose so. But as I'm not her boyfriend, I'm sure she won't mind what I do," he said taking a playful bite on her earlobe.

Jay's lovemaking was urgent, passionate. He kissed and nuzzled every inch of her face and neck, travelling down to the curve of her bosom, deftly unbuttoning the tiny pearl buttons of her shirt as he went. She moaned in pleasure as he slipped her bra strap off her shoulder and his hot mouth sought out her nipple. Gently, he teased her; his tongue flicking the pink rosebud until it was hard and she could stand it no more. His hands moved to her shorts, unzipping them and pulling them down over her slim hips. She cried out as his hands slipped beneath the white lace of her panties and gently caressed her.

Knock, knock, knock.

"Nina, are you all right in there?"

It was Aunt Rosita.

Nina froze.

"Er...I'm fine Aunt Rosita," she shouted, frightened eyes looking to Jay for support. He stayed quiet. "I'm just tired, that's all."

"Can I get you anything?"

"No thank you. Good night."

"Okay, good night."

Nina waited until she was sure her aunt had gone downstairs before she pushed a still amorous Jay away.

"She's gone," he whispered and went in to nuzzle her neck again.

"I know, but that was too close. What if she had caught us?" she said, pushing him away again.

"You're a grown woman, Nina. You can sleep with whoever you want," he said huskily.

"Not under my aunt and uncle's roof, I can't," she said squeezing out from underneath him and doing up her shirt.

"God, you're so old fashioned!" he said playfully. "She's downstairs, she won't hear us."

"I'm sorry Jay, I just can't," she said, suddenly embarrassed. "Please can you go."

He looked hurt, confused, but did as she said.

"Sleep well, Nina," he said as he stood at her door.

"You too, Jay."

Jay was absent from breakfast the next morning and Nina assumed he was still asleep in his room. She sat down and her aunt put a plate of hot rolls in front of her.

"Are you wondering where you friend is?" Rosita asked, a knowing look playing about her eyes. Nina blushed.

"No," she lied.

"He left early. Said he had some business to do. Something about that necklace you were always going on about when you were younger, do you remember?"

Nina paled. So, he was trying to snatch it from under her nose! He was just using her last night to get information.

"Unbelievable," said Nina helping herself to a roll and some home-made jam.

"You know he really is a nice man," Rosita began.

"Who? Jay? You are kidding!"

"Yes, Dr Reynolds. You could do worse." She gave Nina a knowing smile. "And he's a doctor."

Nina sighed. Here as Aunt Rosita trying to pair her off again. She knew better than to try and argue with her. Besides she wanted to get off the subject lest her aunt allude to the nocturnal goings on last night. If Rosita knew what she had been up to, Nina would die from shame, but her aunt said nothing more about it. She stuffed bread into her mouth and tried to dismiss Jay from her thoughts.

After breakfast, Nina borrowed Javier's car again to go and find the mythical centre point. She told Rosita she was going explore the countryside. Her aunt handed her the keys reluctantly.

"I really don't like you running about the island on your own. You should have Roberto with you," she said sternly. "Or Dr Reynolds," she added slyly.

"I'll be fine," Nina said reassuringly. "Besides, Roberto is busy this morning, I'll see him later. And I don't want Jay Reynolds anywhere near me, thanks very much."

"I'd still be happier if you took someone with you. It's not right! A young girl going off on her own."

Nina kissed her aunt on her cheek. "I do it all the time on archaeological digs. I'll be okay. See you later."

There was a freshness in the air as Nina headed briskly to the lockup where the little Citroen was kept. She was almost whistling as she traversed the narrow streets of the old town. She felt sure she would find something today, anything to lead her to the treasure. She turned a corner and came face-to-face with a large man in black. He had a nasty burn scar on his right cheek and smiled menacingly. As she hurried past to the lock-up, she was aware he was watching her every move. Nina fumbled with the keys. She slid the key into the padlock and turned it.

"I wouldn't do that if I were you," a low voice growled.

She spun around to see the man towering over her.

"What do you want?" she said. Her knees felt like they were about to collapse from under her and her heart beat loudly in her chest. "I haven't got any money on me and my passport is at home. Leave me alone or I'll scream."

"I don't want your money or your passport." The man stepped closer. Nina pushed her back against the garage door.

"What do you want then?"

"This," he said yanking her rucksack from her hand.

"No! That's mine!" she yelled just as he punched her in the face sending her spinning backwards into the dust. As she lay there, dizzy from the blow, blood pouring from her mouth, the man ran off. A loud roar, the squeal of tires, and the man and his car were gone. She didn't even have time to get the make or number of the vehicle.

Groggy and disorientated, Nina sat up and touched her face. Her jaw ached and had begun to swell, and her entire body felt sore. She tasted blood. Shakily, she rose and dusted herself off. She needed a brandy and she needed it now. The keys were still in the garage, so she locked it up and made for the safety of her uncle's café.

Clutching her wounded mouth, Nina wasn't looking forward to seeing them. This would only prove to her aunt that she had been right about going off on her own and Nina wasn't looking forward to the inevitable lecture. That was going to be almost as bad as being mugged.

"Oh, merciful Mother of God!" Rosita cried running over to Nina. "What happened to you? Who did this?"

"I had an argument with a man who wanted to steal my bag," Nina said ruefully. She winced as pain shot through her jaw. Where was that brandy? She hauled herself onto a seat nearest to the bar.

"What will Pru think when she hears about this?" Rosita wanted to know. "She'll think we haven't been taking good care of you. Oh! You could have been murdered or raped or worse!"

"Mum won't think anything of the kind," Nina said, "and I wasn't raped or murdered, just mugged."

"I'll call the police," Javier said picking up the telephone. "This is unbelievable. This is unheard of. Alcudia's normally so safe." He shook his head. "I don't know what this world's coming to."

"Can I have a brandy?" Nina asked.

Rosita looked horrified. "A brandy? At this time in the morning? What you need is medical attention." She motioned to her husband. "Javier, go and fetch Dr Alfonso. He'll know what to do."

"No, Aunt Rosita, I'm fine. I just want a brandy to dull the pain."

"Nina Esposito, you will be seen by a doctor and that's that," Rosita replied, shooing Javier on his way.

As Javier left the café, Rosita fumbled about under the bar. Nina asked her what she was doing and she told her she was looking for her first aid kit. A large purple bruise was bearing fruit on her face, Rosita told her, and she wanted to do something about it before it got any worse. Ice. That was what she needed. Nina watched as her aunt went into the freezer and pulled out a large catering bag of ice. Ripping it open, Rosita poured some cubes on to a napkin and brought it over to Nina. She ordered her niece to hold it to her jaw until the doctor arrived. Then she called the police.

Ten minutes later, a young police officer arrived at the café swiftly followed by Alcudia's resident GP. As the cop took a statement, the doctor examined Nina's swollen face. She grimaced as he touched her bruised cheek.

"I don't think anything's broken," he said. "Best get her down to the hospital to be sure, though."

Rosita nodded in agreement. Nina groaned. She had work to do. She couldn't afford to lose any more time.

"I'm fine," she said, "really. It's just superficial. There won't be much the hospital can do anyway."

Rosita frowned. "I think we would be better taking you just to make sure."

"No, that's not necessary," Nina managed a smile. "I'll be okay."

"No, I'm not happy about this." Rosita was concerned.

Nina said: "I tell you what. If I feel my cheek getting any worse, I'll go to the hospital." She told Rosita. "I promise."

She could see there was no point arguing with her niece. "Okay," she agreed reluctantly. "What do I know? I'm only the aunt," she muttered. She stood up and showed the doctor to the door. "Thanks for coming," She added in a lower tone: "Are you sure she's going to be okay?"

"I'm sure."

Nina sighed with relief as the doctor disappeared around the corner. She stood up and made for the back door.

"Where do think you're going?" Rosita asked.

"Up to my room. I've got things to do," Nina replied.

"Okay. Just don't think you're going out on your own again today," Rosita scolded. "It's too much worry."

"I won't."

As Nina began the climb up the stairs, she heard the muffled tones of a man talking in the café. Probably just a delivery man. The sounds of footsteps came from the downstairs passageway then someone called her name. She stopped, heart beating. Who was it? The footsteps raced up the stairs behind her causing to almost collapse with fear. She turned around to come face-to-face with a very strained looking Roberto.

"Are you all right? Oh my God I feel so responsible! I should have been with you today!" He said, barely taking breath. "Look at your face! When I find out who did this I'll tear him limb from limb. I promise."

"It's nothing to worry about, Roberto, honest. Just a bit sore, that's all." She pushed open her door. "I've told the police everything I could about the guy who attacked me. He was quite distinctive, so they may just be able to get him."

Roberto followed her inside. Nina collapsed on to the bed, suddenly feeling very tired. She guessed it was caused by the shock of the attack.

"Did they get away with anything?" he asked.

"Just my bag," she groaned as she laid her head on her pillow. Her whole body was throbbing from when she had hit the ground. She hadn't felt this bad ever.

"Was there anything in it?" He was standing next to the dressing table at the window.

"Like what?"

"You know, valuables?"

"No, not really. Just my loose change and notebook." Her eyes were closed. She needed some sleep. She wished he would just go away and leave her to recover.

"Harper's notebook? Don't tell me they got that?"

She opened her eyes and looked at him.

"No. Luckily I hadn't taken it out with me."

"Where is it then?"

"Why do you want to know?"

"I know how much it means to you, that's all."

She sat up again and sighed.

"It's somewhere safe, that's all you need to know," she replied then said: "Roberto, would you mind leaving? I've had a horrible morning and I'd really like to lie down for a while."

"Of course. Sorry. I didn't think." He leant over her and kissed her forehead. His lips were scorching hot against her skin. She didn't know if she liked the feeling or not. He added: "I'll call in later."

"Thank you."

He was at the door, about to leave, but hesitated. "Are we still on for tonight?" he asked.

"Tonight?"

"Dinner on my friend's yacht. Remember? I can cancel if you don't feel up to it."

Was that tonight? "Of course, I remember." Her hand went to her face. She was self-conscious about the bruising. "I don't know if I can go. I don't exactly look at my best right now."

"It'll do you the world of good. Santana's yacht's amazing. You'll have a good time. No-one will mind about your face, I promise."

"Well...I..." She supposed it would be okay. "All right then. But only if you don't mind going out with someone with a face like mine!"

He looked intently at her. "Your face is perfect," he said softly. He pulled open the door. "See you later then?"

She smiled. "I guess so..."

Chapter 7

NINA woke up four hours later. She tidied her sleep-mussed hair into a ponytail and examined her swollen cheek in the mirror. It was still aching but she was starving and didn't want to go downstairs before she had a shower. The bathroom was next door, so grabbing a huge white towel, she tiptoed naked out into the hallway and across the landing. Nina slipped into the bathroom, snapped the door shut and sighed with relief.

"Well, my!" a voice said behind her.

Nina started then gasped in horror. Jay. Naked in the bathtub.

"I hadn't realised I'd get my own personal water nymph as part of the deal..." The grinning American was lying casually in the clear water and it was all Nina could do to stop herself staring at his naked form. Yet her eyes were drawn to the dark pubic hair beneath the ripples and the mesmerising pink of his manhood. She looked away, horrified at her own boldness. She didn't know what to do, what to say. She felt the heat rush to her face. Realising she too was naked she quickly wrapped herself in her towel and grabbed the door handle.

"Oh, excuse me..." she mumbled, attempting an escape.

"No, don't go!" Jay called. She peeped through the crack in the door. His muscular chest was glistening with water droplets. His hair sleek and shiny. He was smiling at her, beckoning her back in.

"I'm sorry," She didn't know what else to say. "It wasn't locked... I didn't know there was anyone in here..."

He seemed to sense her discomfort and sat up straight, his knees to his chest hiding the raw power that Nina knew was between his legs. She blushed.

"I just wanted to ask you if you were okay, s'all," he said. "What the hell happened to your face?"

"I got attacked when I was out, but it's fine." She opened the door again letting cool air flood into the steamy bathroom.

"You got what? How? What happened?"

"It's nothing to worry about honestly. Just a scuffle at the lockup."

"You shouldn't have gone there on your own!"

"Oh, don't you start. I get enough of that from my aunt."

"Nina, that's terrible. Is there anything I can do?" His concern seemed genuine.

"You know me. I'll live," she said before stepping out and pulling the door behind her.

Back in her room, Nina lay on her bed to collect her thoughts. How embarrassing. How terrible. How hot was he! Stop it Nina! She scolded herself. The last thing you need is to dally with that damned American. Do you not remember what he did to you? What he stole from you? What he's trying to steal from you now? She closed her eyes and tried to clear her head, but all her mind could do was wander back to that toned tanned body lying in the bath just across the hall. He is so handsome. But he knows it. Despite his faults, he's a brilliant archaeologist. He stole your bottle and he's trying to steal your necklace. He's got fantastic eyes.

There was a gentle knock on her door. Nina sat up and arranged her towel around her.

"Come in," she said.

Jay entered wrapped in a bath towel, his hair wet and tousled.

"Are you sure you are all right?" he asked as he came towards her. Nina shrunk back.

"I'm fine," she said, "just a bit shaken, that's all."

"Tell me who did this to you, Nina and I'll hunt him down," he said earnestly. He sat down beside her and put his arms around her. She shrugged him off. "What's wrong?" he asked seeming genuinely surprised. "I thought you and I..."

"You thought wrong," she said.

She gazed into his eyes expecting to see ...she didn't know what, but she didn't expect to see the hurt that was there. He leaned towards her.

"Nina," his voice was hoarse. "I don't understand..."

"What don't you understand Jay?" she asked quietly. "I came here to find something and that something wasn't love or lust or whatever it is you think we have."

"Oh!" he said pulling back.

"Please can you go now," she said. "I need to freshen up."

"Sure."

He stood up and went to the door. He made to say something but must have changed his mind for he departed without another word. Nina lay back on her bed and sighed. She was glad he was gone.

One shower and two hours later, Nina was ready for a night on a billionaire's yacht. She had chosen her evening attire carefully, opting for a stylish white dress and white leather mules. Her hair was piled on top of her head in a sleek chignon and her makeup was simple yet natural looking. Despite her best efforts, no amount of makeup would cover the dark blue bruise that had spread over the right-hand side of her face so she left it, a badge of crime. She skipped out of her room, suddenly looking forward to getting out of the café for the night, away from Jay, and ran smack into him in the hallway. He was heading downstairs and apologised immediately for being in her way.

"You look gorgeous," he said.

I could say the same thing about you, thought Nina as she surveyed the handsome man standing before her in casual slacks and white shirt.

"Thank you," she said.

"Going somewhere nice?"

"Yes, I am."

"With Roberto?"

"Of course. We're going to meet one of his father's old friends. A Mr Santana. We're having dinner on his yacht."

"Santana?" He seemed surprised. "The millionaire?"

"Yeah, I think that was the name. Why? Is there a problem?"

He was frowning. "No, just be careful, that's all." He stepped aside to let her pass. "Yachts can be pretty dangerous places. Have a good night."

"I will. You too!"

Roberto, looking handsome in a dark blue suit, was holding a bouquet of pink roses when Nina got downstairs.

"What are these for?" she asked sniffing the flowers' light perfume.

"Lovely flowers for a lovely lady," he replied, eyes shining.

Her hand automatically went to her jaw and she flinched as her fingers touched the raw bruise that she still sported. "Hardly a lovely lady," she said, laughing, "but they are lovely flowers, thanks." She gave him a quick peck on the cheek. "I'll go and find a vase for these and then we can go."

She almost walked into Jay as she nipped into the back. He didn't say anything as she apologised and went into the kitchen, but she could feel his eyes boring into her. She wondered why she was finding that both uncomfortable and exciting. Her mind took her back to her bedroom the previous day and the bathroom earlier and she blushed as she ran some water for the vase. That was just a moment of madness, she told herself. Then why do you wish the love making hadn't been interrupted? I'm going out with Roberto. As friends. Maybe we will get back together. I don't need the added distraction of Jay Reynolds. Then stop wishing things to be different, Nina Esposito.

Arranging the roses prettily in the vase, she placed it carefully on the kitchen table, intending to find a proper home for it later. She had trouble with one bud which refused to stand up straight and no amount of arranging would fix it. She decided to leave it. She didn't have time to fool about with flowers tonight.

Roberto was chatting to Jay when she returned to the café. She felt a sudden rush of fear. What were they talking about? Were they talking about her? Did Roberto know about her attraction to Jay? About the kiss? She was flustered as she spoke.

"Ready to go, Roberto?"

"Yes." He held out an arm. She took it gladly.

"See you later, Jay." Roberto called as he steered his date towards the door.

"Have a good time," Jay said, almost sadly. Nina looked round at him. He smiled and waved a little too enthusiastically, mockingly even. She frowned. She didn't know what was going on in his head and she didn't want to know, she told herself. Jay Reynolds was an odd man and she was better having nothing to do with him.

Roberto and Nina stepped out on to the street and made their way to the car park where Roberto had left his car. Santana's yacht was moored at Port de Pollenca a few miles to the north of Alcudia and within ten minutes driving.

"So, what's Mr Santana's yacht like then?" she asked Roberto as they turned a corner into the car park. A look of pure joy and longing came over his face. He sighed with the thought of it.

"She's a real beauty," he began. "Sixty feet of pure loveliness. Leather seating and oak trim inside. Fully equipped bar and galley. Her own crew. Just perfect."

"And are we the only guests tonight?" She hoped not. She hated being the centre of attention. Everyone always wanted to know if she lived like Lara Croft or Indiana Jones: uncovering fantastic relics in temples and caves full of booby traps and murderous tribesmen. Nothing could be further from the truth. More a life of dusty books and painstaking research.

"No. It's funny. Jay was just telling me he got an invite to the yacht as well, which will be great for you." Nina flinched. Jay was going to be there? "You two can regale us with all your tales of dare-doing and treasure hunting. Mr Santana is really interested in your search for Aelia's necklace. I think he'd like to help."

"You told him about my work?" She snapped. "It was supposed to have been a secret." She didn't want anyone to know about it in case they got there first.

"He knows everything about Mallorcan history. He's really interested in the history of his people." Roberto replied, anxious to make things right. He looked sheepish. "He might be able to help you," he ventured. "He gives a lot of money to the local museums."

"How dare you tell him about my search!" she growled, "and I don't care how much he gives to the museums, this is my work and it's up to me to tell people about it. Not you. How could you let me down like this?"

"I'm sorry. I didn't think." He motioned to take her hand, but she pulled away and folded her arms across her chest. "I'm sorry Nina, I really am. Honest."

She looked at his pained face and sighed: "Okay. But don't tell anyone else. It's none of their business!" She added quietly: "Especially Jay Reynolds."

He looked at her, shamefaced: "Okay. I'm sorry."

"Where's the car?" she demanded. He pointed to a red two-seater soft-top MG sitting under the shade of a tree. She looked surprised. "I hadn't realised teaching paid so well," she said. "Maybe I should think about taking it up."

Roberto walked proudly over and patted the bonnet.

"This," he said. "Is years of hard work and hard saving. She's my baby." He pointed his key at her and the lights flashed. "Taxi for Esposito!" he joked, holding open the passenger door.

"Thank you, kind sir," she joked back, his earlier indiscretion forgotten.

"Where too Ma'am?" He said leaping into the driver's seat beside her.

"Santana's yacht!" she laughed. "And step on it!"

Chapter 8

JOSEPH Harper's Diary - 6th September, 1979

I've spent most of the day lying at the pool wondering about Manuel's words. What did he mean "it lies directly in the middle of the three places Aelia loved the most"? What would a young Roman noblewoman enjoy doing? Where would she go? What people would she meet?

Have started dreaming about her. Beautiful tragic Aelia. Fell asleep on this chair earlier this afternoon and slept for about two hours. Mary said I slept so long because I had been exerting myself too much with fairy tales. She never understood the fine line between documented history and legend. She says she's worried about Jack. He says he never sees his dad these days. I told her how could he say that? I brought them on holiday, didn't I?

I met a young businessman, Costa Santana in the bar later that day. He was drinking brandy at the bar when I went to order drinks for us. He greeted me and inquired whether or not I was on holiday. I told him we were, but I was also here to do some research on the legend of Aelia. He seemed really interested in what I had to say. A little too interested. So, I gave him the basics, but didn't tell him I was pursuing a new lead.

This is my project after all, not his. My Aelia. My necklace.

The sun was beginning to set and the sky was turning a pretty pink. As Nina got out of the car at the Port Pollenca, she took the opportunity to look around at the stunning scenery. To the north-east, the jaggy outcrop of the Formentor loomed over everything. A craggy peninsular at the most northern part of the island, it was one of the island's beauty spots and home to the gleaming white Formentor lighthouse. She smiled as she took in its majesty, remembering when, years before, she and Roberto had once picnicked there. A cool salty breeze was blowing and Nina felt happy in the company of her former lover. Despite all that had happened today, she was looking forward to dining on a real live millionaire's yacht and living the highlife a little. She felt like a Hollywood princess as they drew up to the gangplank where Santana's captain was standing to meet them.

"Good evening sir, madam," he said as he doffed his cap. An older distinguished looking man, he led them up the narrow gangplank and opened a polished wooden door into the plush interior of the yacht. "Mr Santana asked me to show you into the main reception room. He'll be with you in a moment."

"Thank you," Roberto said motioning for Nina to enter first. Too busy rummaging around in her bag for her lipstick to see him, Nina walked right into Roberto, dropped her bag and spilled its contents out on the deck. A mascara wand rolled purposefully away from her.

"Dammit!" She hunkered down to pick up the assorted lipsticks, packets of paper hankies, pens, mascara wand and keys. Laughing with embarrassment, her eye was caught by a familiar tall figure in black disappearing into a door further up the yacht. She frowned. He looked like… no surely not…

Roberto looked at her quizzically.

"What is it Nina?" he asked. "What's wrong?"

"I'm not sure, it's probably just my imagination," she began. She looked back to where the man had disappeared. "But, I could have sworn I just saw the guy who attacked me earlier."

"What? Are you sure?"

"That's just it, I'm not sure. I need to get a better look at him," she said. "Hold this a minute, will you?" She thrust her bag into his hand and went after him. Yanking open the door, she almost ran into a well-dressed, well-manicured man of diminutive height in his 60s. He had slicked black hair that gleamed in the lamp light and sharp little eyes that twinkled with amusement.

"Miss Esposito, I presume?" He said graciously, bowing slightly displaying a thinning hairline that was obviously dyed. She was too busy trying to look around him to fully take in everything he was saying. She was desperate to get another look at the man in black.

"Eh?" she said trying to peer around the stranger. "Sorry, I was just…"

"Nina!" Roberto warned. Nina looked at him and then back at the man, realising how rude she was being. He was holding out his hand and looking bemused. She took it and shook it firmly. "Nina Esposito."

"I guessed as much," he smiled, eyes twinkling. "Costa Santana."

Her attention switched to him. So, this was the great Costa Santana. He was everything she had imagined. Small, well built with a welcoming air about him. He wore a stylish light-coloured linen suit and sandals, no socks. He wore a simple gold band on the middle finger of his right hand. His dark eyes were gleaming.

"Mr Santana! Thank you very much for inviting us to dinner. I've been looking forward to meeting you," she said. Trust me to run into Santana when I was somewhere I shouldn't have been, she thought to herself.

"And I, you. Roberto has told me a lot about you."

"He has?" She wondered when Roberto had done all this speaking. He had spent the majority of his time in her company.

"Oh yes. He speaks very highly of you." He offered her his arm. "Would you care to accompany me to the main reception room? I believe there is champagne chilling there. Would like a glass?"

"That would be lovely." Giving one last look down the dark passageway, she took his arm. The passageway was empty.

"Are you looking for someone?" he asked turning to see what she was looking at.

"I thought I saw someone I recognised on your yacht. I'm probably mistaken. There's no way he could be here. It's probably just the shock of this." She indicated her bruises.

"Yes, what a terrible, terrible thing to have happened. Roberto told me about it earlier. Were you very badly hurt?" he asked.

"Just this," she replied touching her face. "It's nothing really, just a slap. Thankfully they didn't get away with anything much. I'll just have to be more careful in future." She gave him a nervous smile. "So, champagne is it? Lovely."

Santana led Nina back to the ornately paneled reception room and found her a glass of champagne, French, of course. He would never have anything else, he told her. He greeted

Roberto warmly and motioned for them to be seated on a huge white leather sofa then placed himself in an enormous matching armchair opposite. He lit himself a Cuban cigar, talking all the while as he offered his guests one. Nina declined, Roberto dug right in.

Nina couldn't help but take in the beautiful room. Against the walls were long wooden tables, Spanish Nina thought and old, adorned with expensive-looking lamps and antiquities from ancient times; a marble bust of Julius Cesar, a beautifully crafted bowl and some small sculptures of Minoan bull fighters. On the walls were oil paintings of famous naval battles including, Nina was amused to see, one of Trafalgar.

"So, do you like my yacht?" Santana asked just as Nina took another sip of her champagne. The bubbles fizzed into her nose and she sneezed before nodding dumbly. Santana smiled. "She's a real beauty, isn't she?" He drew deeply on the cigar. "I had her 'specially made by a boatyard near Athens. Cost a fortune, but she was worth it."

"What's she called?" Nina asked.

"I called her The Anna-Maria, after my mother." He replied. He was quiet for a while, seemingly remembering. "She was lovely, my mother," he said. "Just like my yacht."

He added: "Would you like a tour before dinner?"

"That would be great," Nina said eagerly.

Santana pulled a gold pocket watch out of his waistcoat and looked at it.

"My other guests should be here soon. Would you mind waiting and then I can show you all round together?" He slipped the pocket watch back into its place.

"Other guests?" Nina was interested. She was relieved she and Roberto weren't the only people dining with Santana tonight.

"Yes, you may have heard of one of them."

"Oh yes?"

"Dr Jay Reynolds. I believe he's in the same field as yourself." Santana sucked on the cigar, studying Nina's reaction. Her heart flipped a beat and she blushed.

"Yes, we're both archaeologists. Dr Reynolds is actually staying at my aunt's café."

"Dr Reynolds and I may be doing a bit of business together," Santana explained. "I'm a great lover of history and artefacts and while Dr Reynolds was on Mallorca, I simply had to meet him. I've read many of his papers. He's a fascinating man," he continued, barely taking a breath. "I'm looking into the possibility of funding a new expedition to uncover the ruins of some Roman villas on Menorca. Dr Reynolds has been giving me some advice on the matter."

"Roman villas?" Nina was interested. Jay never mentioned this.

Roberto blurted out: "Nina's been carrying out her own expedition while she's been here."

Nina shot him a look to be quiet, but too late.

"Ah yes, Roberto's been telling me all about it," Santana studied her carefully. "You're searching for a lost Roman necklace, I believe?"

"Yes, that's right." Nina felt uncomfortable talking about this. She didn't want anyone else knowing. Damn Roberto for telling.

"Any luck?" He casually blew a grey-blue smoke ring into the air.

She felt a little downhearted: "I've been following up a few clues, but nothing so far."

"That's a real shame," he replied. Then he sat forward. "Nina, may I be frank with you?" She nodded. "I would like to help. I would like to provide you with the money and expertise to find your treasure. I will give you 50,000 Euros to begin with, more if you need it. How does that sound?" He was sure of himself, was certain she would accept his generous offer. She was momentarily taken aback.

"That's a very tempting offer," she began. "And I thank you very much for it." She took a breath. "But, this was something I wanted to do on my own. Can I have some time to think about it?"

Roberto gasped. "Are you mad? Mr Santana's just made you a very generous offer. It could help you solve the mystery." There was anger in his voice and Nina wondered why he was so passionate about it.

She turned to him. "Roberto, this is my project and it's up to me who I want to involve. I do appreciate the offer, but I'm doing fine on my own." She was firm.

He pointed to her swollen cheek: "Really? Are you really fine? That tells me differently. You could use some money to hire yourself bodyguards. Then maybe you won't find yourself being attacked again."

She was flushed with anger. Through gritted teeth, she hissed: "Roberto, let's not talk about this just now. You're embarrassing me."

"Not as much as you've just embarrassed Mr Santana," he snapped.

Santana held up a hand. "Please, I did not mean to cause any trouble. If Nina does not want my help, that's up to her, Roberto."

"But it's so generous," Roberto continued.

"It's fine. The money will always be there for her if she wants it."

Nina managed a smile. "Thank you. I do appreciate the offer and I promise I will think about it."

There was a knock on the cabin door breaking the tension and a steward entered.

"Dr Reynolds and Mrs Almovar have arrived, Mr Santana," he said.

"Show them in!" the host said jovially.

Jay was looking cool and handsome in his casual slacks and short-sleeved shirt. He winked at Nina as he walked in, causing her to look away and blush. She felt like a schoolgirl. She felt like she wanted to run away and hide. What did she think she was doing yesterday by being so brazen? He must think her a right tart. She couldn't look him in the face. At his side, the stunning beauty of Francesca only magnified Nina's discomfort and she found herself feeling more than a little envy. Francesca was clinging on to his arm as if to ensure he would never leave her. She smiled warmly at Nina and Roberto. Nina forced her face to smile back but was annoyed with herself for feeling so conflicted. What had she been thinking? It was obvious Jay was with Francesca. He had assured her that they weren't together, but the way they acted together implied otherwise. They seemed like such a perfect match and Nina was sure he had lied about his relationship as he had about everything else. With a pang of despair, Nina realised there was no room in his heart for her. It was Francesca who had Jay. He was hers. Nina flinched and her heart was as heavy as stone. She had no claim on Jay Reynolds. The incident in the bedroom had been a one-off. It hadn't meant anything, she had told him that. So why do I feel so bad? She wondered.

"Are you all right?" Roberto asked, worried.

"I'll be fine."

"Shall we go in to dinner?" Santana, sensing a slight atmosphere, decided to act. "Please, follow me."

He led the way through double doors into an oak panelled dining area. A huge polished Regency table was laid, with silverware and crystal glasses, for five guests. Cream candles threw a soft light from a silver candelabra in the centre of the table.

"Please, be seated," Santana told his guests, taking his place at the head.

"Are those Monet?" Nina asked indicating the beautiful paintings on the walls. Santana seemed pleased.

"Only copies," he said. "The originals are hanging at my home in Barcelona." He picked up a little silver bell and rang it. The steward appeared.

"Sir?"

"We're ready to start," Santana ordered. The man gave him a short bow and went back into the depths of the yacht. He reappeared a short time later, accompanied by two other stewards carrying bowls of soup and a breadbasket. To her embarrassment, Nina's stomach growled in hunger. Across the table, Jay heard it and smirked. She scowled back.

"My speciality," Santana explained. "Mallorcan bean soup, made to my own mother's recipe."

The soup was delicious and the five hungry diners wolfed it down greedily. It was followed by a fruit course, a main course of roast duck and Spanish vegetables and a fine apple tart to finish off. Over liqueurs, Santana passed round a cheese board and cigars for the men. Jay declined. Roberto again dug into the cigar box eagerly.

"So, what sort of business are you into these days Mr Santana?" Roberto asked casually. He placed the Cuban cigar in his mouth and waited for Santana to light it with a huge gun-shaped lighter.

"Still the restaurant business," Santana said. "For my sins," he added dolefully.

"Things not going so well?" Nina enquired then immediately regretted her thoughtlessness.

"Not as good as they should. Too many people eating fast food these days, nobody wants quality," Santana grinned. "Still, business isn't too bad. I get by."

"Don't let Mr Santana fool you," interjected Jay. "He's one of the top business people in Spain." He smiled at his host. "All this poor business stuff is just a front to make us feel sympathy for him."

Santana laughed.

"Caught!" he said. "I knew I could never fool you, Dr Reynolds."

Jay replied: "You can't kid a kidder, Mr Santana. Did no-one tell you that?"

Santana studied him carefully for a moment as if weighing him up.

"Would anyone like a tour of my yacht?" he said leaping to his feet with sudden enthusiasm. They all accepted the invitation. Nina was especially keen to go. The figure of her attacker was still haunting her and she was desperate to search the yacht. Santana offered her his arm and she took it. Followed by Roberto, then Francesca and Jay, the pair led the way down a narrow passageway. Santana threw open a cabin door. Inside was a beautifully carved desk and a Captain's chair. A flat screen computer sat on the otherwise bare desk.

"My office," he said.

Another door revealed a second sitting room with a wide screen television and a sound system. Another was the guest bedroom. Further down the hallway and Santana stopped outside the double doors of his own cabin. He threw them open and the party gasped as one. Inside was a huge ornately carved wooden bed and matching bedroom furniture. One room off to the right led, Santana told them, to his en-suite bathroom and his steam-room. To the left was the door that led to the Jacuzzi.

"I like my little luxuries," Santana said by way of explanation.

Keeping her voice casual, Nina asked: "So where do the crew sleep?"

"Below deck," came the reply, "but you don't want to be going down there."

"Oh, but I would. I'd like to see the entire yacht," she said enthusiastically, adding: "It's so beautiful."

He patted her arm. "It's just small cabins and the galley. Nothing special."

"No really. I love boats. I'd love to find out how everything works."

"Really?"

"You know us archaeologists. We're always asking questions," she nodded enthusiastically.

"Oh, but I couldn't risk you getting your lovely dress dirty. It's all engine oil and dirt down there." He turned to the rest of his guests. "Upstairs is the bridge." He made towards the door explaining that he would prefer to take them up to the bridge via the deck. Nina hung back.

"Nature calls," she said casually. "Could you tell me where the ladies' room is?"

"You may use mine, my dear," he grinned. "We'll see you up on deck then?" Nina nodded. Santana looked at her for a moment as if trying to make her out. Then he led the rest upstairs. Nina walked casually into the cool marble bathroom, keeping up the pretence, and, once she was sure everyone had gone, peeked outside. There was no-one around. She slipped out of Santana's cabin and made her way down the hallway. She counted the doors: the guest bedroom, the sitting room, the office. Ah! Now where does this one lead? Tucked down at the end of the hallway was a door Santana had skipped during the tour. She tugged it open and peered inside. A brightly lit spiral staircase led down into the depths. She had another quick look around before closing the door behind her and beginning her descent. The sound of her high-heeled shoes clicking down the metal spiral staircase echoed across the confined space and she was relieved to reach the bottom. Another door met her, oval-shaped like those on a warship. She slid the catch and slowly pulled the door. It led into a dimly lit hallway and there was no-one around. It took her a few seconds before her eyes adjusted to the light difference. Then, heart thumping loudly, she tiptoed into the passageway and began to gingerly make her way down the corridor. The muffled sounds of male voices could be heard behind a door at the far end of the corridor and it was towards this she went. The men were laughing and joking with each other and as she drew closer, she began to make out what they were saying. The door was ajar and she could just make out some figures.

"What's Santana doing entertaining these people?" said one in Catalan. "Who's he trying to kid?"

"I know. He reckons he's a toff hob-nobbing with all these fancy people," said another.

"He should remember who he is," a third interjected. "He came from the gutter like the rest of us." The sounds of agreement went all round.

Then the first voice said: "He's getting way above himself. He's scum like the rest of us and he should remember that."

Nina peeked into the doorway, straining to see who was speaking. This was the galley and there were five men inside. Two were obviously kitchen staff with their starched white coats and hats, the other three were casually dressed and were eating sandwiches. The one standing closest to the door turned in profile. Her mugger. She gasped, realised how loud it was and jumped away from the door. The sound echoed down the passageway causing the men to look up. One placed his hand in the inside of his jacket as if to feel for a gun. Another made to step forward.

"What was that?" he asked.

"Nothing," one of the chefs said. "We hear noises down here all the time."

The man wasn't convinced.

"I think I'll just go and check anyway."

He drew a gun from an underarm holster and walked slowly towards the door. Fearful of being caught, Nina desperately looked around for somewhere to hide, but in the darkness of the little corridor, there was none. There was only one thing for it. She stepped forward and knocked the door.

"Hello? Anyone there?" she called, popping her head round the door. The man with the gun hastily hid it behind his back. He scowled at her. "Sorry to bother you," she said. "But I think I'm lost. Could you tell me where the toilet is?"

"Back upstairs Miss," he growled menacingly.

"How do I get there?" she asked innocently. She looked at the other people in the room. The man who had attacked her had his back to her and was pretending to study a newspaper. One of the chefs smiled warmly at her. He took her arm and led her back out into the passageway.

"Go back upstairs and Mr Santana's room is the third on the left. You'll find his en-suite in there."

"Thank you."

Internally sighing with relief, Nina marched back to the spiral staircase. She turned and gave the chef a small wave as she stepped into the stairwell, right into the path of another man.

"Where have you been?" It was Jay.

Nina jumped.

"Jay! You gave me a fright!" she said, squinting in the bright light.

"What do you think you were doing down here?" he demanded. He seemed angry.

"What's it to you?"

"A yacht's no place for a woman to be clambering around."

"What are you talking about? I got lost." As the words left her lips, Nina knew he would never believe her.

"Bullshit. What were you doing down here?" he demanded.

Nina came clean.

"If you must know I was looking for that guy who mugged me. He's on this yacht, Jay. I saw him earlier and he's here! In the galley! I've got to go and find Santana and tell him," she whispered excitedly.

"I wouldn't do that."

"Why not?" He drew closer to her and said in a low voice: "Mr Santana's not the kind of man you want to mess with and neither are the people who work for him."

"But that man assaulted me and stole my bag!"

"Nina, trust me. Santana is dangerous. Your best bet is to say nothing. That guy'll only deny it anyway. Besides are you sure it's the same man?"

"Yes."

"And do you have any witnesses who'll back you up?"

She was crestfallen. "No."

"Then I wouldn't go rocking this particular boat. The police will only laugh at you. Santana's an important man on this island. You don't want to go embarrassing him. Especially when you have no proof it was his man who mugged you."

"But then he'll get away with it."

"Yes," said Jay steering her towards the little staircase. "He probably will."

"What are you doing down here anyway?" she demanded.

"Looking for you!" he said. "I knew you were up to something, so I hung back to wait for you," he said. He grabbed her arm. "Now let's get back to the rest of them before they realise we're not there."

They went up in silence. Nina first, moody and lost in her own thoughts. She knew Jay was right about the mugger, but it still niggled that there was nothing she could do. At the top of the stairs, she reached for the door handle, only to be grabbed at the wrist by Jay. He spun her around. She looked at him quizzically. He smiled back.

"Nina, before we go back to the others, can I speak with you?" His voice was gentle. "It's important."

"Yes, okay. I wanted to talk to you as well." She turned to face him fully. She was afraid of what he might say, of the rejection he was no doubt about to give her. She wanted to get in first.

"You do?" He was looking intently into her eyes and she could see the desire for her was still there. Her own body ached for him, but she knew it could never be. He was Francesca's.

"If it's about yesterday, it's okay," she mumbled as she lowered her gaze. "I won't tell Francesca. I know it meant nothing. It'll be our little secret." She looked up at him.

"Oh right..." He seemed disappointed. Then: "Francesca? I'm not with Francesca," he said, a smile played about his lips.

"Really? You're not? Come on. This is the second time I've bumped into you and her on a date! Do you really think I'm that stupid?"

"She's my cousin," he said. "Her husband is away on business at the moment which is why he's not been with us. We haven't seen each other in a couple of years and we've been catching up. It was she who suggested going to the Festa when she heard I was going to Alcudia and she offered to be my date for tonight. She's been dying to see inside a millionaire's yacht. That's all."

"Oh," said Nina. "Right! So, you're not with Francesca." She felt relieved and then checked herself for being so. *He's after your necklace, dummy, don't forget that!* She scolded herself.

"Isn't that what I just said? I'm not with anyone...at the moment."

"Right." She reached out and pulled open the door. "Good," she said and she slipped into the hallway. He frowned.

"Just a minute! I haven't finished talking to you yet." He followed her into the hallway. She was smiling. "What about you?" he asked.

"What about me?"

"Well… Roberto."

"What about him?"

"Are you with him?"

"No. We're just friends." She looked at him. "Why?"

"No reason." He took her arm and guided her down the hallway. She could see a smile playing on his lips.

"So yesterday really meant nothing to you?" he asked.

"Um, well only if it meant nothing to you."

"It meant something," he confessed, staring straight ahead and not looking at her.

"Good," was all she was giving him.

He looked at her and smiled.

"Is that the best I'm going to get?" he asked. She nodded, grinning. "Well, that's fine for now." He patted her arm. "I think the others are on the top deck. C'mon, we've been away long enough."

The small party had moved outside to take some air and enjoy the cool moonlit evening. Francesca was giggling with delight, peering through a brass telescope mounted on the top deck. Santana had his arm around her pointing out the various constellations, explaining what each one was and the stories behind them. They didn't notice the arrival of Jay and Nina until the pair were standing right next to them. Roberto did.

"Where have you been Nina?" he demanded, a slight note of anger in his voice.

"I got lost trying to find you all," she smiled. "Luckily I bumped into Jay." Her eyes met her fellow archaeologist's and she blushed. The colour in her cheeks was not lost on Roberto. He took her by the arm and pulled her gently to him. His arm slipped easily around her waist and he gave her a squeeze.

"After this morning I thought something horrible had happened. I couldn't bear it if..." he whispered. "You're special to me, Nina."

"Don't you worry about me, Roberto. I can take care of myself," she said. "Besides, nothing happened. I got lost and Jay found me. End of story."

She released herself from his hold and swung over to where a tray of ice cold white wine sat. She whisked up a glass and drank deeply. The sharp crispness of the wine sent her taste buds into overdrive and she licked her lips with the pleasure of its tart gooseberryish flavour.

"Hmmm, this is lovely," she said to Santana. "What is it?"

"I'm glad you approve. Perhaps Roberto would like to fill in," Santana replied. "It is a family make after all." He motioned for Roberto to speak.

Roberto lifted a glass and held it to his nose. He inhaled, eyes closed. Glass to lips, he drank.

"I would say it was one of my father's Sauvignon Blancs," he said. "The '63?"

"Bravo! Spot on!" Santana clapped. "Now would anyone like some coffee or brandy?" He asked his guests.

"Actually, I would like some more of this!" Nina held up her empty wine glass. She was feeling all warm and cosy inside; finally relaxed, at home, all the anxiety and stress of the day suddenly sliding off her and she wanted to enjoy herself some more.

"Don't you think you've had enough?" Jay, who was standing next to her, whispered.

"No. Do you? This is only my second glass."

"Please Nina, you need your wits about you here," he whispered, his breath hot against her cheek.

"So, you've already said," she hissed, "but I can't see it. Mr Santana seems perfectly lovely to me."

"There's 'seems' and 'actually is'," he said. "Besides, you've had a head injury and I don't think drinking too much would be good for you. Plus, don't forget you had some codeine. You shouldn't be mixing painkillers with drugs."

"What are you? My mother?"

He looked sternly at her. "If I was, I'd give you a damned good hiding!"

"All right, I get it! I'll make this the last glass," she assured him.

It was 2am before Nina finally got to bed that night. Giddy with the wine and painkiller mixture, she loped drunkenly into the café and tripped up the stairs to her room with the assistance of Jay holding her up on her feet. Giggling, she let him plonk her down on the bed and kiss her lightly on the forehead before he retired to his own room.

Roberto been angry when Jay had offered to take Nina home, taking it as some sort of insult to his manhood. He had brought her, he said, so he should take her home. Besides, hadn't Jay come with Francesca?

"I'm sure Francesca wouldn't mind if I dropped her off first and then took Nina home, would you Fran?" His date shook her head. "It makes sense, Roberto. We could share a taxi and that would allow you to go straight home."

"I will accompany Nina back to the café," Roberto was adamant. "It is out of the question that you take her."

"But I'm staying at the cafe myself. What does it matter who takes her home, so long as she gets there safely? I mean, look at her."

Nina felt all eyes on her and she was suddenly wishing she had not partaken in any wine. Her eyes were rolling in her head and all she wanted to do was sleep. "She needs to be looked after."

"Exactly and I will do the looking after!" Roberto insisted.

Nina sat next to Santana, laughing jovially as the two men locked horns.

"Stupid men," she giggled.

"Perhaps the lady should decide?" Santana proffered. Roberto and Jay looked at her. She snorted with laughter.

"I don't care," her words were slurred, "so long as I get there."

"I'll take you home, Nina," Roberto was at her side, roughly pulling her to her feet. "Come on."

"Ow! That hurt! All right I'm coming." She turned to Santana. "Thank you for a lovely evening and the lovely, lovely wine."

"No problem, my dear. I hope I may have the pleasure of your company again soon," he said smoothly. He stood up to see them off the yacht. Taking Nina's arm, he whispered: "You will reconsider my offer, won't you? I can be very generous you know. It would make your task a lot easier."

Although a little slow with the alcohol, Nina still had some wits about her. She was gracious in her refusal.

"Mr Santana, you have been generous enough already, but I will certainly keep your offer in mind."

"That's all I ask." He took her hand and kissed it lightly. "Farewell, fair lady."

Roberto held her by the elbow as they negotiated the gangplank. Nina slipped a couple of times en-route to the jetty, giggling at her mis-steps. Roberto wasn't in such a happy mood.

"Why did you have to refuse Mr Santana?" he snapped. "He's one of the most influential men in the Mediterranean. You should have taken him up on his offer."

They reached solid land. Nina shrugged him off.

"Look Roberto, I make the decisions about this," she growled, "me, not you and not Mr Santana. Yes, his offer was generous, but what does he get out of it? I want to find this necklace on my own. I don't want some backer coming in and taking all the glory. This is my search and it will be me who gets any accolades for it."

She stomped off towards the car. He followed her.

"But you've deeply insulted a great man!" he called after her. She pulled open the passenger door but he slammed it shut before she could get in. "You've made him mad."

She inhaled. "He didn't look mad to me," she said. "In fact, he was very gracious." She tried to push him out the way, he wasn't for giving in.

"He was angry. And now that's it for me."

"Wait. What do you mean?" Her hands were on her hips.

"You're not the only one who needs help, Nina. I wanted Mr Santana to help me with a business opportunity. I need his backing. Now it's all ruined because you turned him down."

"It's not ruined because of me." She looked at him, disgusted by his attempt to blame her. "You could still approach him."

"No, it's too late." He closed his eyes as if trying to contain his temper. "It's too late."

"Don't talk crap," she spat the words out. She didn't need this right now. All she wanted was to go to sleep in her own bed.

"Nina, please reconsider. For me, please. If you let him help you it will look good for me."

She looked at him. Hadn't he heard a word she'd said?

"Oh. Well, in that case I should do whatever you say!"

"Yes! Yes, you should!"

"Not a chance, Roberto. Why do you need backing from Santana anyway? Isn't that what banks are for? Do you owe him money or something?" she goaded him. His lips tightened.

"Right, okay. If you're going to be like that, that's fine, but I don't have to listen to it." He growled, moving quickly round to the driver's side of the car he jumped in. Before she could do anything about it, he started up the engine and without even looking back at her, sped off into the night leaving her, aghast, on the jetty. She suddenly felt cold.

"Listen to what?" she shouted after the disappearing car. "Bastard!"

She shivered.

"Can we offer you a lift?" It was Jay. He was peering out of the taxi window. Francesca was at his side.

"Yes," she whispered gratefully. "Please."

Chapter 9

JOSEPH Harper's Diary - 7th September, 1979
Wives are such nags. Mary has been on and on at me for days to do something 'family' orientated with the boy. She says he needs his father in his life. I looked at him playing happily with the other children in the pool. He looked all right to me. I asked her what she wanted me to do with him? She told me to take Jack out on one of those pedalo things. He's only eight. I asked: is that wise? She told me I'd better do it. Reluctantly, I obliged and took the little chap out in the bay. It was actually rather good. Gave me the chance to have a good think about Aelia and where she might lie. Bought a map of the island on the way back to our hotel. Thought I might have a good look at it tonight and then return to Alcudia tomorrow. Mary's reluctantly agreed so long as she and Jack can come with me. So long as you don't nag, I told her.

Had that dream again. She was kissing me. I felt aroused. First time in years that's happened.

Nina felt surprisingly bright that morning considering the wine-painkiller mix she had the night before. She awoke at eight but did not get up immediately preferring to lie on for half an hour to think about last night. She was angry and hurt at Roberto for abandoning her at the harbour. She was furious at him for telling Santana too much and she was irritated at the way he tried to force her to accept Santana's offer. Why was he so concerned about it? Oh, Roberto. You have some explaining to do, she thought. She closed her eyes for a moment, readying herself for the task ahead: today, she vowed, she would start her quest afresh, with no men, no money offers and no distractions.

The bathroom was empty. No Jay in the bath this time. She locked the door behind her and steeled herself to look in the mirror. Her face still ached and she hoped some of the swelling had gone down. She walked bare-footed across the cool tiles to the shaving mirror and looked. One half of her face was a palette of blues and purples and greens.

"My, you're looking lovely this morning, Miss Esposito," she said aloud. "Why, thank you ma'am," she added in a faux Texan accent. "God, I look bad," she groaned. She went to the shower. She may look like she's gone ten rounds with Mike Tyson, but at least she would be clean.

Forty minutes later and Nina was in her own room putting the final touches to her makeup and hair. Dressed in a vest top and shorts, she wore her hair up and off the back of her neck, it was cooler that way. No amount of concealer was going to cover up that corker of a bruise, so Nina just left her cheek au naturel with the rest of her face. She put on a touch of moisturiser with sun block and dabbed her face with a little powder to take off the shine. A couple of flicks with the mascara wand, a dab of lip salve and she was ready to take on the world. She grabbed her hat and slipped some money into the pockets of her shorts. After breakfast, she was going down to the market to pick herself up a new bag. She missed her battered old rucksack and hoped she would be able to replace it with something similar.

In the kitchen, she found Rosita singing softly to herself as she poured coffee for her husband. Uncle Javier was sitting at the table reading a paper. He smiled warmly at his wife as she put a steaming mug down in front of him. There was no sign of her cousins or of Jay Reynolds. The kitchen was peaceful, happy, and Nina almost didn't want to interrupt this domestic bliss. Javier saw her hesitate at the door.

"What you doing standing there in the doorway, girl? Come on in and get yourself some breakfast," he called.

Nina took her place opposite him at the table. Rosita sat down beside her.

"Now, first thing's first," she said to her niece. "What would you like?"

"Just some coffee, please, Aunt Rosita," she replied. Rosita frowned.

"Just coffee? No breakfast?"

Nina nodded.

"You must have something. If only to help your poor body recover from that," she pointed to Nina's bruised face. "How about some toast? You'll have some toast."

Nina relented. "Okay. Toast would be nice."

Rosita smiled: "You must look after yourself Nina."

"So everyone keeps telling me…" she sighed.

As Rosita made the toast she kept glancing back at her niece, a smile playing about her lips. Nina frowned for she knew what it was all about. Rosita placed a plate of toast and the butter dish down in front of her niece and smiled warmly. There was an aura of waiting about her aunt, waiting for Nina to spill the beans on something. Nina did not take the bait.

"Are you going to keep us in suspense?" Rosita asked. Her curiosity was just too much for her.

"About what?" Nina asked knowing full well what her aunt wanted to know.

"How did last night go? Did you and Roberto have a good night?" She eyed her niece looking for clues as to how the younger woman felt about her old flame. "Did he treat you well? Was there romance?"

Nina shrugged.

"Or maybe it's that blond doctor, Jay, you like best," Rosita said. Stop fishing, Nina thought, her face crimson with embarrassment.

"No, there is no romance between me and Roberto or Jay Reynolds for that matter either," Nina said. "And there never will be," she added regretfully, thinking of Jay.

"Why not? They are both handsome boys," Rosita said with a grin. "And you're not getting any younger," she added.

"Leave the girl alone," Javier said. "If she wants to tell us about her love life, she will in her own good time."

Nina looked at her uncle and smile. Thank you, she mouthed. He replied with a wink.

After breakfast, Nina took Harper's notebook and sat in the café's shaded tables outside. It was a fine morning and the square was already busy. Sipping coffee, she carefully went through the diary entries again. Over the past week she had read over every page several times seeking clues, new insights, but had come up with nothing. She had a sinking feeling that today would be no different. As she flicked through the yellowing pages, her mind wandered to the events of the previous evening. Had she really seen her attacker on Santana's yacht? Yes, she was sure it was him. If so, what was he doing there? Did Santana know he had hired a thug? Her hand went unconsciously to her cheek. Why was Santana so keen to help her? He didn't know her. She could have been anyone. He claimed to be interested in preserving his island's heritage, but something niggled. If Nina had not seen her attacker on his yacht last night, she would never have thought twice about Santana's offer. But the fact made Nina worry. Had Santana instructed the man to mug her? If so, why? What use could her satchel be to a man with the kind of money Santana had? She looked down. A breeze ruffled the pages of Harper's diary. Something clicked. Was Santana after the diary?

"Morning."

Nina jumped. She turned around to see Jay standing next to her. He was smiling. "Oh! You startled me. Good morning."

"Sorry. Can I join you?"

She nodded.

"What ya up to?" he asked looking down at the book opened before her.

She hastily closed it and placed her hands protectively on top of the battered cover. "Nothing that you need worry about," she said.

He looked taken aback. "Only asking," he said. "Boy. Someone's touchy this morning. Is that because your boyfriend dumped you last night?"

Oh, here we go, she thought. Jay's back to his old sneering self.

"For starters, Roberto is not my boyfriend. Secondly, he didn't dump me last night. I dumped him!" Why was she sitting here listening to this? She thought. She gathered her things together and stood up. "Now, if you'll excuse me, I've got things to do."

She walked smartly off into the small square, conscious that many curious eyes were staring at her and her purple face as she went. She heard footsteps behind her and Jay darted out in front of her. He grabbed her arm.

"Oh Jay! You gave me a fright!" She was still shaky from the attack earlier. "I thought you were…"

"Sorry, I didn't mean to scare you," he said.

"What do you want?" she asked trying to free herself from his grip.

"Look, Nina, I got off on the wrong foot with you again," Jay said releasing his grip. "I'm sorry. I know I was out of order. I was trying to be funny, but it kinda backfired on me. Sometimes I can't help being cheeky. I'm sorry." He held out his hand.

She looked at it, sighed and took it. "Okay, but no more boyfriend quips," she replied. He grinned.

"What've you got there?" he asked. Nina was suspicious. She hadn't forgotten what he had done in the past. She held the book tightly to her chest.

"A notebook."

"Whose?"

"It belongs to me."

"What's in it?"

"Jay, I don't mean to be rude, but I'm not going to answer your questions."

"Why not?"

"Because quite frankly I don't trust you."

"I'm not going to take your necklace from you, I promise," he said. "And maybe I can help."

He moved towards her. She pulled back.

She was firm. "I've already told you. I don't need or want your help. Now, if you'll excuse me, I've got work to do." With that, she turned on her heel and strode off in the direction of the market, leaving Jay, mouth gaping, behind her.

Alcudia market stretched from the town square through the narrow, cobbled streets and out to the old town walls. Covered stalls jostled for space, groaning under the weight of items that might attract tourists: leather belts, purses and wallets; traditional woven carpets and carved wooden figures; caps, hats and T-shirts emblazoned with 'I love Alcudia'; watches, jewellery and hair adornments; pottery and ornaments. Right at the end, next to a stall selling dolls was what she was looking for: the leather bag stall. The stallholder jumped to attention when he saw her approach. Hungry for a sale, he embarked on his sales patter in English.

"You like bag?" he said holding up a fake Gucci. Nina shook her head. He put it back down.

"Have you got any rucksacks or satchels?" she asked. "Let me see." The stallholder rummaged under the piles of handbags and pulled out a small russet-coloured rucksack. "This?"

She examined it, then shook her head. He dived into the pile again and dragged out a larger satchel. It was a dark brown leather that gleamed in the sunlight and felt soft to touch.

"How much?" she asked.

"For a pretty lady like you? 100 Euros."

"Fifty."

"Lady, you try to rob me! 100 Euros."

"Sixty."

"Ninety Euros."

"Sixty-five."

He thought about it for a moment. "Ninety Euros," he said. Nina sighed and shook her head.

"No, too much," she replied and turned away. She could hear him muttering to himself.

"Lady! Okay! We have a deal!" he shouted after her. She turned to look at him. Smiled.

"Sixty Euros?"

"Aw, c'mon. What you trying to do? Put me out of business? Sixty-five Euros!" he grinned. She returned the smile. "Okay."

Nina shifted the notebook onto one arm and reached into her pocket for some Euros. She counted them into the stallholder's hand then took her new bag. Looking up to thank him she caught sight of the scar-faced man at the street corner, talking to another man. He saw her looking and scarpered.

"Hey!" Nina shouted as she ran after him. "Hey, you!"

She got to the corner just in time to see him duck into a familiar black limousine. It drove off at speed just as Nina ran towards it.

"I knew it…" she said to herself. "Santana is behind all of this!"

Roberto was sitting at the bar when Nina got back to the café. She didn't particularly want to speak to him and stuck her nose in the air as she went to walk by. He was not for letting her go.

"Nina," he stopped her. "Can I speak to you?"

"I'm busy, Roberto. Got stuff to do."

"Please, just for five minutes. I wanted to tell you that I'm sorry I was so jealous last night. I'm sorry I left you."

"Jealous? Of whom?"

"Jay," he said almost indiscernibly. "I thought he was getting a bit too friendly."

Nina blushed. "And why would you think that?" she asked quickly. "What difference would it have made if he was? You and I are no longer an item, remember? We were over a long time ago."

"I know, but...well, it was just hard seeing another man drool all over you like that," he said. He shrugged. "I suppose forgiveness is out of the question?" He turned his big brown eyes on her. In the past, that would have been enough for her to melt into his arms, but she was older and wiser now. She didn't have the same old feelings for her former love. She liked him, but that was it. She smiled to herself, pleased with this revelation. She hadn't fallen back in love with him after all, as she had feared she would.

"I suppose I could forgive you...this time."

"That's great!" he said grabbing her arms. "And I suppose a little kiss is out of the question?"

"You suppose right!" she said, extracting herself from his grip. She headed to the back of the café, hesitated, and then turned to face him again. She was suddenly serious. "Look, Roberto. I don't think it's such a good idea you helping me with the search."

"But..."

"It's been great seeing you and everything, but I really feel I want to do this on my own." She was firm.

"It's because of Santana, isn't it? I pushed you too much." He seemed gutted.

"A bit." She held out her hand to him. "We can still be friends. We can meet up later if you like."

"But what about the man who attacked you? He could try again. You need protection. I can protect you."

"He got what he wanted: my bag and my purse. I don't think

he'll be back for any more. Not now. I'll be fine," she reassured him. She turned to leave. "See you later."

She waited until Roberto had gone before going outside again. Armed with her new rucksack, a map and sturdy walking boots, there was a spring in her step as she strode out of the café and into the street. She finally felt she was doing something useful – without the help of Roberto or the distraction of Jay. Church bells somewhere struck 10am and the temperature was a perfect 70. She smiled and hummed a little tune to herself as she walked outside the old city walls, certain that in a short while she would finally find the site of Aelia's tomb.

Nina had estimated that the 'centre point' of the places Aelia loved was about three miles outside the new town. She had pinpointed it on the map and was desperate to go there and see if she was right. She strode to the taxi rank, jumped in a cab and asked the driver to take her close to the field where she believed lay more clues. As she settled into the back, the door opposite her opened and before she could protest, Jay slid in beside her.

"What do you think you're doing?" she blustered.

"Coming with you," he replied.

"But you don't know where I'm going."

"Even more reason to come. You need a protector and I'm the man for the job."

"A protector? I don't need anyone. This is my show and I don't want you interfering in it, okay? Now, if you don't mind - I'd like you to get out of the taxi and go away." She was more than irritated.

He folded his arms. "I'm not going anywhere," he said. "You're stuck with me for the rest of the day."

"I know what you're up to, Jay. You're out to steal from me again." She was outraged.

He sighed. "Don't be stupid. I just want to make sure you're okay."

She snapped: "I'm fine. Now leave me alone."

The taxi driver, tired of the rumpus, turned around: "Lady, do you want to go or not?"

"Not until this man gets out of your taxi!" she fumed.

The driver turned to Jay. "Are you leaving?" Jay shook his head. He made himself more comfortable in the back seat. The driver focused back on Nina. "He's not leaving. You still want to go to the field?"

She nodded. There was no way she was going to allow Jay to stop her. She would just have to ignore him that was all. She turned away from him, pretending to be fascinated with the streets outside. Jay leaned over and touched her leg. She jumped.

"Don't you dare!" she said. He took his hand back.

"Sorry. Look Nina. I just want to make sure you're safe. I don't want you going wherever it is your going and then something happens to you. I would never forgive myself if it did."

She looked at him quizzically. "What do you care?"

"More than you think." He changed tack: "Besides, I think you're secretly pleased I'm coming along with you."

"You think wrong!"

"I'll be good, I promise," he joked. "You'll hardly even know I'm here. Besides, you could always do with an extra pair of hands. If we don't find anything, then maybe we could think of something else to do." He waggled his eyebrows comically and grinned. She couldn't help herself; she laughed. He was right. If anything went wrong no-one would know where she was.

Yet should she trust him? He seemed determined to follow her anyway. Then: "Okay. I suppose I'm just going to have to put up with you."

Jay smiled.

"But don't think you're in charge!"

He held up his hands. "Never," he said.

"And don't think I won't be watching you!"

"For what?"

"I know you, Jay Reynolds, don't forget."

"Jay Reynolds?" The taxi driver shouted from the front. He glanced round. "THE Jay Reynolds. The archaeologist?"

"Yes?" Jay seemed surprised.

"I loved your documentary on Queen Nefertiti," the man said. "It was great. Very interesting."

"You saw that?"

"Oh, yes. We have satellite television. Great show. Are you planning to do anymore?"

"It was supposed to have been a one-off, but I'm open to offers."

"When did you do a television programme?" Nina asked.

He leaned over and murmured: "Oh, I'm full of surprises, Miss Esposito. As you may learn some day."

She groaned and turned away. Big headed bastard, she thought. She stared out of the window for the remainder of the ten-minute ride while Jay and the taxi driver chatted amiably about ancient history. They journeyed out into the countryside and in no time, the car had drawn up beside a field of tinder dry grass.

"Here we are. This is where you wanted to go," said the driver.

"How much do I owe you? asked Nina.

"Eighty Euros," replied the driver.

"What? We've only driven for 10 minutes."

"This is the middle of nowhere! Look, I'll do you a deal. You can have the ride on the house on one condition. You give me your autograph, Dr Reynolds." He added: "And a photograph?" He waggled his phone.

Jay smiled and drew a pen from his pocket. "Well, I'd be delighted."

"Good. God!" exclaimed Nina. "I think I might be sick…"

Nina rolled her eyes, impatient to get going.

"It's for my son," said the man handing Jay a piece of paper. "He's a big fan."

Jay took the paper. "What's his name?"

"Carlos."

Jay scribbled something on the paper and handed it back to the driver. He seemed delighted. Then the two men put their heads together whilst the driver took the picture. He was beaming as the camera in his phone clicked.

"Thank you!" He shouted as he started the car. "Adios!"

"Adios!" Jay waved back. "It's always so nice to bump into fans…" He turned to Nina and saw she was already trudging across the field. He shouted on her to wait, but she either didn't hear or was ignoring him. He bounded over the little wooden fence that separated the field from the road and ran up to her.

"Nina, wait!" he shouted.

With an audible sigh, she stopped in her tracks and turned to face him.

"If you must tag along, then hurry up!" she shouted back. "I don't have all day, you know."

"Oooh tetchy! I love my women strong," he joked.

"I'm not your woman," she replied. Her stomach did a flip as an image of them together, making love on her bed flashed through her mind. She pushed the stupid idea to the back of her head. She wasn't going there again. Not now. Not ever.

"That may change," he said, almost imperceptibly.

She ignored the comment and walked on.

Tramping across the bed of scrawny grass and weed, Nina was determined to find something, anything, in the middle of this scorched patch of land that would lead her to her trophy. She marched on, Jay at her heels, her eyes scanning the dry land for a sign, something that would tell her she had made the right decision in coming here. Failure didn't bear thinking about. She couldn't stand the thought of Jay Reynolds thinking she had made a mistake, that her famed archeological training had foundered and all her hard work had been in vain. She reached what she guessed was the middle of the field and came to an abrupt stop. Jay stopped too. One hand shading her eyes against the setting sun, Nina scoured the land for traces of a burial or Roman artefacts. There were none. All she could see for miles and miles was the burnt fields of Mallorca and the dusty grey curves of the main roads.

"Why are we here?" Jay asked. "There's nothing here."

"Shhhh," she said. "I'm trying to think." She looked down at the ground and scuffed around a bit. Kicking up only bits of stone and dust, Nina began to despair of ever finding a clue when her eyes alighted on a slightly raised piece of ground some ten paces away. She walked over and crouched down. Pulling back the grass, she discovered an ancient grating.

"Jay, come here. Look what I've found," she said excitedly.

Jay didn't seem as impressed. "It's an old well, so what?" he said. "It'll be getting dark soon, shouldn't we be thinking about getting back?"

"No, not yet. This is a clue," she said. She grabbed hold of the grate and pulled. "Come and give me a hand moving this."

"Why? What's so interesting about an old well? I'm sure there are hundreds all over this island," said Jay.

"Just help me, will you?" she snapped.

He bent down, his hand lightly brushing hers causing her to shiver. Ignoring the sensation, Nina continued to heave and together they pulled the rusting iron grating away from the top of the well. Nina reached inside her satchel and pulled out a torch. Shining it in, she could just make out the bottom of the pit and to the left, a rusting metal ladder. Handing the torch to a protesting Jay, she swung her legs over the side and cautiously put her weight on the top rung of the ladder. It held.

"Nina, what are you doing? You'll hurt yourself."

"Just pass me the torch, will you?" She held out her hand. He shoved the torch into it.

"Nina, don't go down there. Why don't you wait until later and we'll come back with proper ropes and climbing gear?"

"Nope, got to do this now," she said stepping down the ladder. "I've got to see if I'm right. I won't be able to rest until I've looked."

The top of her head was now the only piece of her showing. Now there was nothing. Only the metallic sureness of her footsteps descending the well indicated she was still there. Jay sighed and stood motionless at the top. Nina's head popped up again.

"Thought you were here to look after me," she called up. "Aren't you coming?"

He hesitated then nodded.

"Can't let you have all the fun, can I?" he said as he manoeuvered himself into position over the top of the well.

The climb down was surprisingly warm, not damp, and Nina

reached the bottom in minutes. She held the torch up to allow Jay to see his way down and once he had reached the bottom, she swung its beam around to have a look. The torch scanned the red clay walls, picking out the odd spider's web and a dried skeleton of a once thriving plant. There seemed to be nothing unusual about the tunnel except for its lack of water. Its dry walls and mustiness made it obvious there had been no water here in many years. Nina lowered the torch beam and behind where Jay was standing found what she was looking for: a large round grate big enough to let an adult through. She passed the torch to him, grabbed the grate and gave it a mighty heave. With a squeal the metal the guard came off easier than she anticipated and the force of the pull coupled with the weight of the metal caused her to fly back and hit the other side of the well. She fell with a whump onto the hard earth.

"Are you all right?" Jay went to help her up.

"Yes, fine. Nothing damaged except for my pride. Get this thing off of me, will you?" Nina pushed the heavy grill away from her and was relieved to get out from under its weight. She allowed Jay to pull her to her feet and, ignoring the thrill that was ringing through her at his touch, grabbed the torch again. "C'mon. Let's go explore."

"Nina, we don't have the proper equipment. Let's come back tomorrow."

"Is the great Jay Reynolds scared?" she teased.

"No, I just think it would be better to let someone know where we are in case something happens."

"I just want to take a look. Then we can come back. Don't be such a big scaredy cat."

"I'm not. I'm just looking out for you, is all."

"Look, Jay, I didn't ask you to come, you followed me. If you want to go back, go back, but I'm going on."

"I followed you because you're a headstrong little minx who needs taking care of," he said angrily. "And this latest escapade just proves that you need looking after."

"I do not."

"Damn right you do!"

They were almost nose-to-nose and Nina could feel the heat of his body against hers. Her mouth felt dry and her heart beat faster. He smelled great, all masculine and warm and dusty from the climb. She felt an overwhelming urge to kiss him, but he got there first. Pulling her to him, Jay bent down and kissed her hard on the mouth. She did not resist but gave over to the heavenly sensation of the embrace. She closed her eyes and allowed herself to be swept away by pleasure.

The kiss ended with a soft peck and a smile from Jay.

"Now will you come back to the café with me?" he murmured as he nuzzled her neck. Her skin was alive with his touch and she nearly agreed to his request, but her own stubbornness cut in.

She pushed him away. "No!" she said and wriggled free from his grip. "I'm going on."

Without saying another word, she adjusted her rucksack over her shoulder and stooped to enter the pitch-black tunnel. She heard Jay curse in frustration and smiled when she heard him follow.

The tunnel had obviously not been used for a long time. Dust and cobwebs created sticky curtains across her path forcing Nina to push through them with her hands. "Jay, look at this," she said as she examined the walls of the tunnel. At the start it had been cut out of the earth and plastered with rough clay; now it was decorated with red clay tiles. Nina ran her fingers over the smooth varnish. "These would have been expensive in their day."

"Whoever built this would not have put tiles in it if there wasn't something special at the end of it."

Nina felt her heart leap into her mouth. "Come on!"

Nina hurried down the passage, the torch swinging wildly all over the tunnel as she ran. Unable to see properly, she did not realize the way was blocked until she ran smack into a wall.

"Ouch!" she cried as she bounced off it and fell to the ground, the torch rolling out of her hand.

With a chuckle, Jay helped her to her feet.

"I told you that you couldn't look after yourself," he said.

Nina scowled at him, but in the dark the look was lost. She picked up the fallen torch and shone it on the wall blocking their path. It been expertly built; the bricks tightly packed and cemented together with mortar with was no sign of any weaknesses. She sighed with disappointment.

Holding her hand up against the wall, she said: "I can't believe this. I was sure we were so close. Damn it!"

She suddenly felt tired and slide down the wall to the cold ground. Tears of frustration and disappointment pricked the back of her eyes. Jay ran his hands over the grainy bricks.

"We'll need proper tools to get through this," he said. "A couple of days work, I reckon. And we'll need some help."

"Will I do?"

They both jumped at the sound of the disembodied voice. Nina swung the torch around to see who had spoken.

"Who's there?" she sounded panicky, frightened.

"I thought you of all people would have recognised my voice..."

Nina gasped.

Roberto emerged from the shadows.

"What are you doing here? How did you get down here?" Nina was shocked and she was too stunned to be angry with him.

"I followed you and Jay to the field. I watched you climb down into this… sewer. I thought you might need my help, so I came after you." He turned to the wall. "Nice handiwork," he said, admiringly. "It's going to take a lot of work to break through that. Do you really think the lost treasure's in there?"

Nina had been wondering that herself but wasn't about to admit that to Jay and Roberto.

"Yes," she lied.

There were a few moments of silence between them as each contemplated the historic riches that may lie behind the wall. It was Jay who spoke first.

"C'mon," he said to the others. "Best be getting back. We can't do anything until tomorrow. It's nearly lunchtime and I hear my lunch calling." He patted his belly which growled on cue.

"No need," Roberto replied smiling holding up a heavy rucksack. "I've got some things in the car that we could maybe use to break through that wall. Give me a minute and I'll go and get them."

"What…?" said Nina surprised.

"I know you Nina," her former lover smiled, "I know you just can't leave things alone, so I borrowed a few things from a friend."

"What friend?" Jay wanted to know.

"Does it matter?" Roberto answered a little too defensively. Then his voice softened. "Do you want me to go and get them or not?"

"Yes," replied Nina still shocked at his thoughtfulness. "Roberto…" she began.

"I know!" he grinned. "I'm a star!"

Before she could reply, Roberto was off down the corridor.

"That wasn't what I was going to say," Nina muttered. "It's just not like him to be so…thoughtful." What is he up to? She wondered.

"I suspected that myself," Jay replied. "I mean, who would be sensible enough to bring equipment on a treasure hunt?" he added sarcastically.

"Okay, so I came to see what was here and I didn't bring any tools," she said under the embarrassingly glowing shine of his amusement, "but I didn't expect to find anything!"

"Apparently!"

"Anyway," said Nina rallying, "Roberto did think to bring some supplies and that's a good thing."

"Right!"

Roberto returned to them ten minutes later sporting what looked like a brand-new rucksack filled with shiny tools: varying sizes of pickaxes; some brushes and a few plastic bags for samples. There was also a torch, six small bottles of water and a few granola bars.

"Are we okay to go?" Roberto asked handing Nina a pickaxe.

Chapter 10

"WE should take out a couple of the centre bricks and work it back from there," Nina said finally. They had been debating how to take down the wall for some fifteen minutes. Nina was keen that there should be as little damage as possible. Roberto didn't care. "What do you think Jay?"

"Sounds like a plan," the American answered testing out the weight of one of the pickaxes. "Step out the way and I'll give it a try."

"No need," said Roberto pushing forward with the largest of the pickaxes. It was as long as Nina's arm and topped with a ferocious looking double head. Nina thought it looked more suited to a building site. "I'll do it." He winked at Nina and took a swing.

"No!" Nina and Jay both yelled. Roberto dropped the axe.

"What?" he said.

"You could bring the ceiling down on us," said Jay. We don't know how stable it is. No, we need to scrape the bricks out carefully, one by one."

"That will take all night!" Roberto was irritated. "Why did I bother bringing these if we weren't going to use them?" He demanded. "If I had known you wanted to scrape away bit by bit Nina could have used her nail file!"

Nina flinched. She had forgotten how childish Roberto could be.

"Don't worry, we will use them," Jay said. "Just not in the way you planned."

As he spoke Nina examined the mortar under the torchlight looking for the best place to start. She sighed.

"What's the matter?" Jay asked.

"It's just a detail, and it could be nothing," she muttered. "Something's not right about this mortar. It's not Roman."

"Here, let me look," Jay said as he took the torch from her and looked closely. "You could be right. This part here looks more modern."

"Look, you can see where the original mortar has overlapped on the surrounding bricks, but there's a whole patch of bricks in the centre that have been stuck together with something else," Nina said.

"Who would have done this?" Roberto wondered aloud.

"Grave robbers, possibly," Jay replied.

Roberto gasped. "You mean they've already been here and stolen the necklace?"

"Grave robbers wouldn't have bothered to brick it up again," said Nina.

"True," said Jay. "This was done by someone who wanted to cover their tracks."

"There's only one man who would have done this," Nina said in a tone that was almost reverential. "Joseph Harper. He found her. I just know it!"

"Does that mean the treasure isn't here?" Roberto asked anxiously. "And this was all just … what is it you people call it… a wild goose chase? Have we been wasting our time?"

"Well there's only one way to find out!" Jay said. He took his axe and began to painstakingly scrape away at the newer mortar. It collapsed like cake crumbs and within twenty minutes, Jay had his first brick removed. Roberto watched from behind Nina, his arms folded across his chest and lips pursed.

"Perhaps you could hold the light whilst I help Jay," Nina said sensing his dark mood.

"Sure, why not? I mean I was the only one who thought to bring this stuff with me," he mumbled as he took the torch from Nina.

They worked non-stop for about an hour, taking turns to use the pickaxe. Brick after brick after brick came away and before long they had made a hole big enough to poke a head through. Trembling with excitement Nina grabbed the torch from Roberto and shone it into the space beyond. The torchlight caught a flurry of dust as Nina panned it into the darkness. She bit her lip and continued to swing the light around. Her heart was racing as she scanned the hidden room for treasure. Now she knew how Howard Carter had felt when he found Tutankhamen's tomb nearly a century before. She could hardly breathe for the excitement coursing through her body.

"Can you see anything?" Roberto wanted to know. "Is there a sarcophagus?"

"Hold on a minute!" she said peering into the gloomy space. "Let me just look over there." A few moments went by. Then, she let out a sigh of frustration. All she could see was the smooth walls of another chamber. No sarcophagus. No tomb. Nothing.

"It's empty," she said unable to hide the disappointment in her voice. This wasn't going to be as straightforward as she had at first thought.

"Let me see," Roberto took the torch from her hand and peered into the darkness beyond. "I think I see another entranceway," he said. "What do you think Jay?"

"Where?"

"Over there, to the right."

Jay took a look.

"Certainly seems to be. Let's take a ten-minute break before breaking through any more. Agreed?"

"No! We must keep going," Roberto urged. "We're nearly there, why stop now?"

"Why are you so keen, Roberto?" Jay wanted to know as Nina handed him a much-needed bottle of water. He took a swig.

"I just want to see if Nina gets to fulfill her dream," he replied.

"I've waited a long time to find Aelia's tomb," Nina said, "another few minutes won't matter. Let's take a short break and we'll resume once we've had a rest, okay?"

"Sure."

But Nina was on tenterhooks. She was dying see what lay beyond the wall. This was everything she was dreaming of: finding the legendary Aelia and her fabled necklace. After all these years of research and reading, she was on the cusp of solving one of the biggest mysteries of the ancient world. She fidgeted and bit her thumb whilst she waited. She could not sit still so anxious was she to get going. However, she understood Jay's need for a rest. They had been working in tight, cramped conditions. It was dusty and cold and a break would refresh them for the next step.

Ten minutes passed before Nina was back at work chipping away at the brickwork. Half an hour later and she had made a hole in the wall big enough for everyone to crawl through. Nina led the way. Torch shining ahead of her, she squeezed through and, not waiting for the others, scrambled into the chamber.

"Oh my God!" she gasped as she swung the torchlight around the walls.

The temperature was decidedly chillier and she shivered as she stood in awe. The light picked out colourful wall paintings depicting Roman life: on one were female musicians and two women dancing, a second wall was the representation of a bearded poet or playwright (Plato?) and on the third were the images of an older man and a young woman with dark curly hair. Was that Aelia and her father? More excitingly, the torch beam fell on a set of square steps that led up to a raised floor. Beyond it was an arched doorway leading into another room. She could hear Jay and Roberto at her back and paused for a moment to let them catch up.

"Wow," Jay whispered in her ear, his voice full of wonder and excitement. "I think we've may have found her."

"Not yet," Nina replied. "No one's been buried here, but there's another ante-chamber through there that I think we should explore."

"Ladies first," her companion said with a smile. Nina did not need a second invitation.

Forgetting all about Roberto, Nina skipped up the steps and went into the room. Jay was hard at her heels and they saw it first together. She gasped as she looked around the chamber. It was a medium sized room with a white marble floor and a high painted ceiling. The walls were decorated with scenes featuring Roman gods and goddesses, and Nina smiled when she recognized Dionysus, the Roman god of (among other things) the theatre. Standing in the middle of the chamber, beautifully carved with symbols of fruit and animals and wine, was a small stone sarcophagus. Each segment had been exquisitely carved from pieces of white marble by a master craftsman. It was stunning as it glowed in the semi-light.

Trembling, Nina stumbled over and touched the lid. It was ice cold, damp, hard. Could this be her? Had she really found her? She put her torch on the ground and placed both hands side-by-side on the edge of the lid. Giving it a shove, Nina soon found she did not have the strength to move it. "Jay can you give me a hand?"

Together, they heaved and slid the lid to the side. Nina grabbed up her torch and shone it inside. The sight was almost too beautiful to imagine. Lying there, laid out, were the remains of a corpse, ragged robes flimsy and faded. Roman jewellery and pots lay all around her, a coin to pay the ferryman Charon glinted from her open mouth and draped around her neck was a necklace of such beauty that it caused Nina to gasp. It was a bib style necklace made of gold with at least 30 thumb-sized pear-cut amethysts set at angles to look like leaves. Salt water pearls were dotted around the leaves to look like pretty white berries. Hanging down in the middle of the necklace was stunning white opal the size and shape of a hen's egg. It was contained in a basket of gold dripping with yet more pearls. Nina has never seen anything like it before. There was a lump in her throat as she gazed at the grave. She felt teary.

"I can't believe it," she croaked, voice full of emotion. "Aelia."

She reached in, suddenly compelled to touch the woman who had for centuries been hidden from the world. Her fingers gently traced the skull and she wondered what this mysterious noblewoman had really looked like. What colour were her eyes? What did she want from her life? What were her dreams? How had she felt when her love had been killed? Nina's fingers traced the skeleton's jaw and then gently reached for the necklace. She picked up the opal first. It felt heavy and cold and was breathtakingly beautiful. Under the torchlight, the amethysts sparkled enticingly.

"Let me have a look," Jay going to her side. Nina stood aside to let him see. "It's a beauty," he murmured.

"Step away from the casket!" said a voice from behind.

The pair looked up shocked by the harshness of the tone and saw Roberto pointing a handgun at them.

"Roberto!" Nina cried. "What are you doing?"

"What I was hired to do!" he said stepping up to the sarcophagus and glancing inside. Keeping his eyes on Nina and Jay, he put a hand in, felt about and yanked up the necklace. "Roberto! You can't!" Nina screamed as he started to back away. "Think about what you are doing. That necklace belongs to the people of Mallorca!"

"No, my dear Nina, that necklace belongs to Mr Santana now," he replied.

"What?" She couldn't believe what she was hearing. "You bastard!"

"No, let me correct you on that… I'm now a rich bastard," he sneered. "Mr Santana is paying me a lot of money to get this for him. He'll be waiting for it now, so I will say goodbye. I would like to say it was nice seeing you again, Nina, but it wasn't. I thought I was rid of you the last time, but you turned up again like a bad smell. Now, I know you will definitely be out of my life once and for all!"

With that, he turned and fled the chamber.

Nina felt physically sick. Her life's work was being snatched away from her. The dream she had had since childhood was being destroyed by this evil greedy little man. She started to run after him and got as far as the stairs when a small explosion tipped her off her feet. Jay raced to her side and helped her up.

"I guess we now know what he meant by never seeing you again," he said dryly as the dust cleared leaving a pile of rubble where the exit had once been. The way out was well and truly blocked.

"Shit," said Nina wiping the dust from her eyes. She coughed. "What are we going to do now?"

"I guess we're just going to have to find another way out," said her companion waving the detritus from the air around her. "If there is one."

It took less than ten minutes to establish that there was no other exit. They were trapped and no-one knew where to look for them. Nina looked at her phone. No signal. With a forlorn sigh, she sat down on the steps and put her head in her hands. She felt wretched. Not only had she signed her own death warrant but Jay's as well.

"I'm sorry," she murmured as he sat down beside her and put an arm around her shoulders. This time she did not shrug him off so grateful was she for the human touch.

"What for?"

"For dragging you down here. If it hadn't been for my stupid obsession with that necklace, you wouldn't be here," she said, tears welling in her eyes. He reached into a trouser pocket and pulled out a clean linen handkerchief.

Handing it to her, he said: "Nina, I can think of no other place I would rather be at this time than by your side."

"Don't be daft," she sniffed. "This is the worst thing that's ever happened to you. I mean, how are we going to get out of here?"

"It's not the worst thing," he said. "The worst thing that ever happened to me was losing you the first time round. I should never have bought that bottle from under you. I didn't know you were after it, but when I found out I should have given it to you. It was the biggest mistake of my life because it meant I lost you. I had hoped that we could get to know each other better."

She turned her tear-stained face to his.

"Do really you mean that?" she said.

"Yes."

"You're not just being nice because we're about to die?"

"No."

He leant in and lightly kissed her on the lips.

"I've fallen for you Nina Esposito," he murmured and he kissed her on the forehead.

"Now you tell me," she replied tears pricking her eyes.

"I've always had impeccable timing!" he said softly, "usually!"

She smiled. He loved her and…well, she realized, she loved him. They were about to die…what a waste!

"I think I've fallen for you too!" she whispered, suddenly shy. He gave her a squeeze and they were silent for a moment, each lost in their own thoughts and being comforted by the other's body heat. Then Jay pulled away.

"Nina, it doesn't make sense," he said suddenly.

"What doesn't?"

"The sarcophagus." He twisted back to look at it. "How the hell did it get it in here? There's no way they could have got it down the well and along that narrow passageway."

"Maybe the tunnel was bigger and they filled it in?" she said.

"Or maybe there was another way…"

"What're you saying?"

"I'm saying there must have been an alternative route into the chamber."

Nina looked at him, thought about what he had said and realized he was right. The sarcophagus couldn't have been brought down the well and along the tunnel, it was too big, too heavy, too awkward to move. There must have been another way in. She scrambled to her feet.

Nina looked at Jay. Jay looked at Nina. And together they said: "The chamber!"

They hurried to the crypt and began searching for clues. Using the torch to light their way, Nina and Jay carefully went over every inch of wall and floor space until Nina's eyes hurt looking at the never-ending walls. They used their fingers to search along the smooth cold interior. They squatted on the floor swinging the light this way and that seeking out a trapdoor or something that would give them a hint of an entrance. They found nothing. Exhausted, they sat down with their backs against the sarcophagus. Nina spoke first.

"We've looked everywhere, Jay. Face it, we're goners. We might as well make ourselves comfortable and wait for death."

"Do you have to be so depressing?" he said pulling her close to him.

"Sorry. I just never thought I would die this way. I've been looking for this tomb practically my whole life and now I'm going to die here!" She smiled at the irony. "I thought I would live til I'm 90 and go in my sleep," she said.

"It's going to be okay," he said.

"Is it?"

"Someone will come and find us," he added.

"How will they find us?" she wailed. "No-one knows we're here. It could be days before they track down the taxi driver and he tells them where he left us. Then they'll have to find the old well and realise we are down here and by the time that happens and they find us, we'll be dead because we've run out of air."

"Yeah and that'll happen sooner rather than later if you don't calm down," Jay pointed out.

"You don't have to be like that," she muttered.

"Yeah? Well, you don't have to give up so easily," he barked. "We could still find a way out of here."

"We've looked everywhere," she said.

"Well, we'll look again," he replied. He stood up. "Come on, let's try the walls and ceiling again…before the batteries run out in the torches."

Seeing she had no other option, Nina switched on her torch and idly scanned the room again. Its light flickered across the walls like a spectre in the night, finally resting on the mural of the older man and young woman. Nina got to her feet and stretched her stiff legs. Then without really knowing why she was drawn there, she walked over to it. There were many murals in the room, but this was the one that called to her. The man was perfectly groomed and in a white toga, the woman in a dress of blue and her dark curls were piled high on her head. Aelia? Nina wondered. If so, there was no sign of the famed necklace. She looked more closely at the painting and it suddenly struck her that it had not been created to the same high standard as the others. She spent a few minutes comparing it to the other images in the room and was puzzled to discover her theory proved to be correct. It had not even been painted by the same artist, but by someone with far less talent. The styles were even different.

"That's odd," she said aloud.

"What was that?" Jay called.

She looked more closed at the woman in the frieze.

"I'm saying this mural is odd. It's completely different from the others!" she said, tapping the wall. Expecting to hear a dull thud, instead she was surprised when the wall sounded hollow.

"Jay! Come quickly! I think I've found something."

"Listen."

She knocked again, this time a little harder, the force dislodging flakes of the painted plaster. She winced as it fell to the ground, but her feelings for the ancient artwork were dispelled when once again there was the unmistakable sound of a hollow wall. There was a sharp intake of breath from Jay before he spoke.

"You're brilliant Nina!" he said as he walked away towards their bags at the base of the sarcophagus.

"Where are you going?" she asked.

"To get the pickaxe," he said. "I think you've just found our way out."

When it comes to the matter of life or death or even whether to preserve a Roman artifact or oneself, humans will inevitably do everything for the preservation of life. Guilty at the prospect of such wanton damage, Nina photographed every inch of it for posterity. Then the two historians took out their tools and smashed the wall down to reveal a wide tunnel and the wonderful scent of fresh air and the sea. Nina could hardly contain herself. They were saved!

Grabbing their things, the pair hurried down the dark corridor, not caring where they went, only thinking of getting out of the tomb. The tunnel was large enough to allow the tall American to stand up without fear of bumping his head and wide so that they could hurry, hand in hand, towards freedom.

Ten minutes later, they found themselves at the mouth of a cave leading to a tiny beach and the wonderful sight of the sun rising over the Mediterranean.

"We've done it!" Nina gasped, her face lit up with joy. "I can't believe we're alive! I thought…I thought…"

Jay grinned.

"I know…I thought we'd end our days down there too," he said scooping her up in his arms and kissing her hard on the mouth. She responded immediately, eagerly seeking the soft warmth of his embraces.

She pulled away.

"Did you mean what you said in there?" she asked. "About you and me and you loving me?"

"Did I say I loved you?" he asked, suddenly serious. "I don't remember that."

"Watch it, or you'll be facing certain death for the second time today," she laughed.

He smiled and his eyes lit up with amusement.

"I was only joking," he teased, "I did say it and I did mean it. I love you Nina Esposito. Despite the fact you nearly got us killed."

She smiled.

"So, did you mean what you said?" he asked.

She thought about making him suffer for teasing her, but her kind heart wouldn't allow her to.

"Yes, I did," she said giving him a hug.

"Now that we've got that sorted, how are we going to get off this beach?" he asked. "I believe the tide is coming in."

"Is it?" she frowned.

"Yes, my feet are getting wet!"

Chapter 11

HAND-in-hand, they waded out of the cave to the morning tide. Nina looked around in dismay: there was no beach to walk to only cliffs and rocks. They were trapped.

"Now what?" Jay said, exasperated that their escape plans were once again thwarted.

"Now we climb," Nina replied pointing upwards the cliff-face. "Give me a leg up, will you?"

Getting on to Jay's hand and then shoulders was not as easy as it sounded. Nina's tired and aching body just wouldn't stretch and bend enough to allow her to clamber up. Although in her own mind she had the grace and stamina of a gazelle, her attempts were more akin to comedy than the beauty of such gentle creatures. Jay was also tired but managed to stay standing as his companion heaved her leggy, awkward body up.

"Jesus!" he cried. "For a small thing, you weigh a lot."

"Big bones," she huffed automatically. "Besides…nuggghh-hh…five seven's not that small."

"Smaller than me, thank God," he replied balancing the teetering woman on his back. "C'mon, give it some more backbone. You can do it. One last push."

With a mighty grunt, Nina pushed up and found herself

standing on Jay's shoulders, bent over, hands holding on to his strong hands, fearful she would fall. Gently, gingerly, she let go of one hand and stretched up the cliff-face. She grabbed hold of a handhold and let go of him. Without looking down at the waves lapping below, she scrambled up and up, grazing knees, cutting hands and generally having a pretty miserable time until at last she reached the top. She pulled herself over and lay there in the dry and itchy grass, panting and thanking God she had made it. Huffing and puffing from below indicated that Jay was following her and a few minutes later, his handsome tanned face peeked over the edge.

"Nice of you to give me a hand," he said, pulling himself up.

"You didn't look like you needed it," she replied. She sat up, tears of relief stinging her eyes.

"Are you…crying?" Jay asked. He crawled to her and enveloped her in his strong, muscular arms.

"Y-yes," she sobbed unable to control the sudden hysteria that swept over her. "I'm…s-s-sorry I nearly got us killed. It was stupid to go down there. I'm sorry," she wept.

He held her tight and stroked her hair.

"Don't be silly, Nina," he said softly. "I would have done the same thing. Finding the tomb has been your life's passion and you had to go and look for it. Besides, you didn't exactly invite me to come along, did you?"

She shook her head.

"You okay?" he asked as her weeping subsided and she sniffed.

She looked up at him, eyes red and teary.

"Oh Nina," he groaned staring down at her, his eyes liquid with desire. She smiled and moved in for a kiss, eyes closed and lips puckering. "You look terrible!" he laughed, holding her from him.

Her eyes shot open. "Thanks a bunch!" She playfully punched him in the chest.

"Ow! I'm joking," he grinned. "Come here."

And he kissed her; a long, lingering, passionate kiss that only a man in love can give.

And she kissed him back and suddenly all her fears, all her anguish melted away and were forgotten.

"Oh my god!" shrieked Rosita when her disheveled niece stumbled through the door and collapsed on a chair. "We were worried sick about you! Where have you been all night? I was just about to call the police! I thought you had been kidnapped or murdered or something more terrible…like…like… Oh hello Dr Reynolds, I didn't see you there. Come in, come in. Have a seat."

"We're fine," Nina said as Rosita offered Jay a drink. "I'd like one too."

"Thank you for bringing our Nina back to us," she gushed placing a glass of freshly squeezed orange juice in front of the amused archaeologist. "Where did you find her? Had she been drinking? Do you think she has a problem? Should I be worried? I don't know what I would have told her mother if something had happened to her!" she said throwing Nina an evil look.

"Aunt Rosita!" Nina snapped. "I am here you know and I'm not 12. I'm a grown woman, I can be out all night!"

"I was with her all night," Jay said.

Rosita flinched.

"We were looking for the tomb," her niece continued, "and… well…we found it!"

Nina explained what had happened: about her finding the

well and the tomb and about Roberto and being trapped underground; about their subsequent escape. Her words were accompanied by gasps of shock from her aunt. When Nina had finished, Rosita was silent.

"Are you all right, Aunt Rosita?"

"Yes dear, I'm just stunned, that's all. I can't believe Roberto would stoop so low….to you of all people." She sighed. "I had heard he had some problems, but to steal from a friend! It's unbelievable! And then to leave you in there to die! It's…it's…unthinkable."

"What problems?" asked Nina.

"He has been arguing with his father," Rosita began, matter-of-factly. "And it got so bad, his father disowned him. Someone said it was over gambling debts or something, but I don't know for sure." Rosita paused. "I thought he was a nice young man. Just shows you, you can never be too careful."

"Gambling debts? That doesn't sound like the Roberto I used to know." Nina replied, then she remembered how quickly she had been dumped and forgotten, and it suddenly came to her: she had never truly known Roberto.

"I know, it's tragic. The evil drink must have taken hold and forced him to gamble all his money."

"Aunt Rosita," Nina could hardly believe what she had just heard. "How can you say that? You and Uncle Javier own a bar and serve that so-called evil drink."

"Darling Nina. Our alcohol has been blessed by the Virgin herself. Just look how close we are to the church! How can this place be bad when it's in the shadow of the statues of so many saints?" Nina rolled her eyes in disbelief. Rosita continued: "There's nothing evil about the drink we serve. It's all good and spiritual, not like the stuff that Roberto's been taking."

"Who was Roberto in debt to, Aunt Rosita?"

"Some big businessman, I think. Javi thought he might be doing odd jobs for this man."

Nina felt the colour drain from her face. Her aunt could only be talking of Santana. She felt Jay's eyes on her and could see that he was thinking the same thing. Weirdly, though, it was a relief that she had some explanation for Roberto's behaviour.

"Everything okay?" Jay asked, reaching out and putting an arm around her. She smiled.

"Yeah," she replied, snuggling in. There was nothing like a bit strong American to make a girl feel better.

Behind the bar, Rosita smiled knowingly.

Before they could rest or get cleaned up, Rosita insisted Nina and Jay call into the local police office to report the theft of the necklace and their imprisonment. The desk sergeant did not look impressed with their story but assured them he would pass the details on to a detective "as soon as one was free".

"Anyone would think we had made it all up," Jay muttered as they left the tiny police station.

"Santana's got a lot of influence around here," Nina said forlornly. "I hope that doesn't also mean with the local police."

He squeezed her hand. "C'mon," he said. "Let's get you home for some rest. You look exhausted."

"But what about the necklace? Shouldn't we be doing something to try and get it back?"

"Let the police deal with it. It's their job."

Nina slept the sleep of the dead that afternoon. All thoughts of regaining the necklace drifted out of her head as she lay down on the soft, clean pillows and pulled the light blanket over her aching body. She did not awake again until the next morning, making an appearance just as the family was clearing up the breakfast things. Dressed in her pyjamas and housecoat, Nina walked over to the coffeepot on the stove. Yawning, she sleepily poured herself a cup of coffee and took a seat next to Rosita. Javier was sitting in his usual place, reading his paper at the other end of the table. Her aunt laughed at her appearance.

"Well you'd never make the finals of Miss World today," joked Rosita.

Nina's hand shot to her hair, which was clearly in need of a brush. She touched her cheek. She had forgotten about the assault earlier in the week, but the traces were still there. However, the swelling had gone down a good bit and she had only a yellowing bruise to show for her troubles.

"Well, can't look gorgeous all the time," she said. She grabbed a piece of bread and lavished it with strawberry jam. Biting into this delicious breakfast, Nina hardly gave herself any time before inquiring after Jay. Javier and Rosita exchanged glances.

"What?" Nina asked. "What's happened?"

"Dr Reynolds is getting ready," Javier said. His voice was soft and its tone suspicious.

"Oh…okay," said Nina. She had expected him to be already waiting for her in the kitchen so that they could discuss their next move, but she had slept longer than she had intended. She was surprised to find herself feeling upset that he wasn't here to speak to her. Still, he would be down soon. Her stomach did cartwheels at the thought.

"He's getting ready to speak with his fiancée," Rosita added somewhat sadly. She looked at Nina, eyes full of worry. "She's waiting in the café for him."

"What? Sorry? I thought you said…" Nina couldn't have

heard her aunt correctly. "…his fiancée?"

"Fiancée? Yes, that is what I said." Rosita's lips were pursed. "Funny, how he never mentioned a fiancée before," she added.

"Especially not to me." Nina's voice was small, lost. She continued nibbling on her bread, brow knitted in thought. She couldn't taste anything now. How could he have done this to her? She had thought they were beginning to build something special between them. She had trusted him. He had said he loved her and she loved him. The bastard; the lying, cheating, two-timing bastard. Did his fiancée know what type of man he was? Nina doubted it. He had probably hoodwinked her as well.

Nina rose from the table, her chair screeching across the flagstones. Rosita and Javier looked at her, concerned.

"Aunt Rosita, Uncle Javier," Nina said, voice wavering as the devastation of this new information threatened to overwhelm her. "I'm going upstairs to get dressed. I've got stuff to do today."

Rosita nodded.

"And," Nina added, "if you see Dr Reynolds." She paused as she searched for the right words. "Tell him I'm busy."

Nina did not go upstairs directly but peeked into the café to see what Jay's fiancée might look like. She spied a tall, arrogant looking blond sitting in the corner seat at the window. The woman was sipping a cappuccino and flicking her hair. She saw Nina staring.

"Good morning," the woman called. Nina nodded. "Beautiful day, ain't it?"

"Yes, lovely," Nina replied, almost dumbstruck.

"Are you a friend of Jay's?"

Nina stepped into the café, painfully aware of only being

dressed for sleep and, worse, she had no make-up on.

"You could say that," she replied. "And you are?"

"His fiancée, Candy." The woman held out a hand, her perfect nails painted a pearly pink. Nina shook it. The woman continued: "Nice to meet you." A beat. "Is Jay ready yet? I want him to show me the sights. You know, we may just come here on our honeymoon. It's so beautiful here, ain't it?"

"Yes," Nina muttered.

The woman took a lipstick out of her handbag. Holding a compact in one hand, she delicately dabbed her lips a matching pink to her nails. Nina watched her, fascinated. The woman wore too much makeup, her hair was long and loose and she smelled of Chanel No 5. She caught Nina looking.

"Well? Is Jay about ready, or isn't he?" she snapped. "I'm really desperate to see him. Haven't seen him for ages." She smiled. "Be a dear and go and get him for me, would you?"

Nina said nothing, merely grimaced and turned tail. She ran through to the back of the café, tears stinging her eyes. So, it was true, Jay had a fiancée. She quickly climbed the stairs, head full of Jay's treachery.

Deliberately not looking at the traitor's bedroom door, Nina flew into her own room and threw herself on the bed. There was no way she was hurrying Jay up so that he could fly down into the arms of that woman. She was so hurt and angry with him that if she had seen him, she would have smacked him right in the face. Whack. How dare he come on to her and pretend that he had ever wanted to form a relationship with her? How could he have implied that he wanted something meaningful? When he had a fiancée in tow! The poor woman. How many times had he two-timed her, had he done this to her? Suddenly everything became clear to her: all the things

Jay had said to her, all the things he'd done, were lies. Had he really just wanted to help her find the necklace or was he really after it for himself and Santana got there before him? She was so glad she hadn't had sex with him… at least she didn't have to feel the horrible dirtiness and cruelty of a one-sided one-night-stand; the next-day realisation that all he'd wanted was a non-emotional shag and nothing more. At least she didn't have to go through the crawling shame of that.

She breathed deeply. Bastard! She suddenly wanted to have a shower, to cleanse herself and rid herself of the memory of that man once and for all. When she was ready, she would slip out so that she would not have to see the two of them together, downstairs, in her family's bar. Besides, she had plenty to do: she had to know if the police had gotten anywhere with their inquiries, if they had tracked Santana down and recovered the necklace; and she had to phone George and tell him the news that the necklace had been found and ask him to try and find out if Santana had tried to sell it yet. She had so much to do. She didn't have time to think of that two-timing bastard and his blond haired bint!

Her head was buzzing.

"Nina!" Aunt Rosita called from the kitchen. "Telephone call for you!"

"Who is it?" she snapped then immediately regretted her tone. Nina didn't want to be bothered this morning and she didn't want to go back downstairs in case she ran into Jay or his soon-to-be wife, but that wasn't Aunt Rosita's fault. "Sorry," she called.

"It's a Detective Henri."

"Right." Nina ran down the stairs and took the receiver from her aunt. Breathlessly, she said: "Hello?"

"Dr Esposito," Detective Henri said. "I'm glad I got you. I'm just ringing to let you know that we are not following up your complaint."

"What?" She couldn't believe it. "Why not? Senor Santana hired someone to steal a necklace. Aren't you going to do something about that?"

"Senor Santana denies all knowledge of your necklace," Henri said firmly. "He says he did not hire Roberto to steal anything. Senor Santana claims you were making the whole thing up to make him look bad."

"He what...?" Nina could feel the familiar heat of anger growing inside her body. "But all you have to do is send someone down the well and you'll know Dr Reynolds and I have been telling the truth."

"Dr Esposito, I have no doubt that you and Dr Reynolds were carrying out some sort of excavation," his tone was patronising. Nina frowned. "but, we have insufficient evidence to take this case any further. It's your word against his."

"Not quite. Dr Reynolds was there too. Doesn't his statement mean anything?" she spluttered, anger rising in her throat. "On Santana's orders, Roberto Hernandez left us in those caves to die. He took that necklace and left us down there. Why won't you people do something about that?"

He sighed: "Dr Esposito, I'm sorry, but Senor Santana claims he was at a cocktail party in Palma at the time and doesn't know this Roberto."

"But Roberto confessed."

"I'm sorry, Senorita, but without more evidence, there's not much else we can do," the policeman said. "Senor Santana has now left the island. We had no cause to keep him here. We will keep the case open, I promise you. In the meantime, my officers are out looking for Roberto."

"So," she growled. "You're just going to let Santana get away with one of Mallorca's greatest treasures?"

He said nothing.

"Fine," she said and slammed down the phone. "I'll just have to go and get it myself."

Santana's magnificent yacht was still in the harbour. She parked Javier's car and marched over to where the boat was docked. One of the crew, a small Spaniard, was on the quayside, unloading boxes from a van. She idled over to him and gave him her sweetest smile. He ignored her and heaved a flat box of pineapples on to his shoulders. Swinging around, he made for the gangplank, Nina dancing along beside him.

"Excuse me," she said. "Is Senor Santana on board?"

"Dunno senorita," the man said grabbing the railing to steady himself.

"Is there anyone I could ask?" she asked hopefully.

"No, sorry, everybody is busy."

"Busy? Are you leaving?" Maybe she could find out where they were going and follow them there.

He stopped his tracks and turned to look at her.

"Why do you want to know?" he said, his eyes drinking in her slim figure and pretty face. She shuddered. "Maybe we can come to some arrangement."

"What sort of arrangement?" she asked carefully.

"Oh…I don't know…" He ran a finger along her wrist and up her arm. It was all she could do from recoiling in disgust.

"I don't think so," she growled pulling her arm away.

The man shrugged and turned his back to her. He swayed as he walked up the gangplank. Nina watched him in dismay.

Now she would never find her necklace now.

"He's going to Amsterdam," a voice said from behind her. She spun around to see a steward standing there. He was a small man of around 40 with kind eyes. "And won't be back on Mallorca for at least a month."

"Thank you," she said.

"You're welcome madam," he replied. "Now if you'll excuse me, I have to go aboard."

She stood back and watched as he embarked. Amsterdam, that makes sense, she thought, he'll be going to sell the jewels on the Black Market. Nina about turned and walked swiftly towards the car. She had a plane to catch.

Chapter 12

THE airport was noisy with tourists pushing trolleys laden with bright yellow carrier bags of booze and over-stuffed suitcases. Great armies of holidaymakers, their tans peeling from their shoulders, waited impatiently at the check-in desks as their children shrieked and chased each other. Nina sighed at the sight. She hated travelling with other people. She hated the pettiness of their shunting and pushing to prevent anyone else from getting into their place in the queue. She hated their brats running around shouting at the tops of their voices, their parents diligently ignoring them as they annoyed everyone else. She despised their gaudy football tops and their fat feet squeezed into nasty little sandals or trainers. She took one look at the check-in desks and was glad she was not returning home straight away. Instead, she made her way to the KLM desk and inquired about flights to Schiphol Airport.

"The next isn't until 6pm," the Dutch sales rep told her in perfect English.

"That's fine, I'll take it." She rummaged in her rucksack for her purse.

"Single or return?" the woman asked, not looking up from her computer screen.

"Single." Nina handed over her credit card.

Within minutes, the ticket firmly gripped in her hands she thanked the woman, picked up her suitcase and dragged it to a left luggage office. A small café selling hot snacks caught her eye. She nipped inside, ordered a bacon baguette and a glass of beer and found a table. She had a few hours to wait until the flight, might as well make herself comfortable.

She dove into her satchel and pulled out Harper's diary. Well, Joseph, you were right all along, she thought. I did find Aelia and I did find her fabulous necklace. And I also lost it… Her heart sank as she thought of it in Santana's greedy hands. She flipped through the pages and began reading the final entries in the book.

17th September, 1979

This is the end of my search for now and I'm having a hard time thinking about how I am going to raise the money for a second expedition. Mary thinks I'm crazy, that the necklace does not exist, but I know it's out there, somewhere, hidden from thieves and bandits. The Romans were terribly clever fellows when it came to burying their valuables. I hope, not too clever in this case. I feel I'm very close to finding it and it's frustrating that we are returning home to rainy old London tomorrow. I'm quite depressed about the whole thing. Planning to see Reg over at the museum as soon as I can. He'll know who to approach for a grant. Meanwhile, must keep plans quiet from Mary. She's worried people might think I'm losing my marbles over this quest for Aelia's treasure. I tell her 'maybe I am' and she doesn't laugh, merely calls me a 'silly old fool'. I hate it when she says that.

3rd February, 1980
Am bitterly disappointed with reception to new expedition. I really thought I knew who my friends were, but not one has come forward with the readies. Mary says it's because they all know, like she does, that the necklace is merely a legend. She says it's the Holy Grail of Mallorca and I said she was being stupid which led to another huge fight. Some of my so-called friends - although I would not even call them acquaintances now - have even gone so far as to write to the papers and journals telling the world and his mother of how foolish I'm being searching for something that doesn't exist. Reg even laughed in my face, right in front of the Board, when I suggested he might want to come on the search with me. I thought he was right behind me. How wrong can a man be? Am planning to fund second expedition on own. Mary is furious with me, but it has to be done. Am sure she'll understand.

Here the diary ended, except for a loose sheet which fluttered on to the tiled floor of the café as Nina flicked through the book. She stooped to pick it up. It read:

10th January, 1981
Have just returned from second trip to Mallorca. I'm deeply regretting going. The publicity I generated before the trip seemed like a good idea at the time - it did help me raise some of the funding after all - but am ruing the day I made my quest so public. Have come home to derision. Everyone is laughing at me. Mary has done her 'told you so' speech to death. We're not getting on. Looks like curtains for the old marriage. I will write up a full report of this second quest later, too tired at the moment.

"Having fun?" Jay sat down beside her. Nina slipped the

loose sheet back inside the diary and turned on him.

"What are you doing here?"

"Looking for you," he said calmly. "I thought I had missed you."

"I bet you did!" She drew her eyes off him, unwilling and unable to look at him. She felt sick. Her head was pounding and it was all she could do to stop herself running away from him, but she wouldn't give him the satisfaction of knowing she cared.

"Look, I think I've got some explaining to do," he began.

"Oh, do you think so?"

"Yes." He touched her arm, she flinched. "I think you need to know about Candy."

"Candy, your fiancée? Yes, I think you had better tell me all about her."

"She's not my fiancée, she's my ex-girlfriend," he explained, "although try telling her that."

"Have you told her that?"

"Of course!"

"Right, now you've told me too. Now go. Leave me alone. I'm busy." Nina snapped. She took up the diary again. He grabbed it out of her hand and slapped it on the table.

"Hey!"

"Listen to me," he said firmly. "I'm not finished."

"Why should I?" She looked at him for the first time. His face was drawn, worried. "You lied to me."

"I didn't lie. Candy and I split up months ago. We'd only been seeing each other a few weeks. I hadn't told you because I didn't think it was important."

"Important? You didn't think it was important to tell me you were engaged?"

"I didn't tell you that because we were never engaged. She took the split pretty badly and has been harassing me ever since, wanting to get back together, telling me she's sorry for whatever it was she did. Truth is: Candy didn't do anything. I just didn't love her." He sighed. "Not like I love you." He waited for a reaction.

Nina didn't know what to do, what to say. She looked up at him, her face felt hot, tears were threatening to spill.

"I love you Nina. You're the woman I want to be with, not Candy." He reached over and took her hand. "We split up ages ago. You have to believe me."

He seemed sincere, but she didn't know what to think. Could she trust him?

"So, what's she doing on Mallorca then?"

"She wanted to get back with me, pick up where we left off… you know the sort of thing." He shrugged. "I told her I had met someone else, someone special." He rubbed her hand. He looked directly into her eyes.

It was all too much. Nina blinked back the tears, removed her hand from his and composed herself. She wanted to believe him, needed to believe him, but was he telling the truth?

"Okay," she said after a time. "I believe you… this time." He smiled. She wiped the tears from her eyes. "But what happened to Candy? Where is she now?"

"She's back on a plane to the States," he replied sorrowfully. "I bought her a ticket home and I've just dropped her off at the American Airlines desk. I can't believe she wasted all that time and money coming over here to look for me."

"She must have thought you were worth it."

"Yeah, right."

He was quiet, thoughtful. Nina drew a paper hanky out of her pocket and blew her nose.

"And now, here I am doing the same for you."

Nina laughed.

"You okay?"

"Yeah," she replied with a smile. "I think I am." She suddenly felt calmer, happier. "So how did you know I was here?"

"Who do you think? Your aunt! After you left, she came looking for me, said you were leaving and if I had any sense I would go after you and apologise until you took me back. Said you were a great catch and I was a stupid idiot if I didn't see that."

"What did you say?"

"I said I was a stupid idiot for not telling you right away when Candy showed up..." he began.

"Why didn't you?"

"Cos, like Rosita quite rightly pointed out, I'm an idiot," he replied. "I wanted to see what Candy had to say before I spoke to you. You were fast asleep. I didn't want to wake you... I should have." His voice trailed away. "Anyway, I came straight here expecting to have missed you." He frowned. "The flight for London has left," he said. "Why weren't you on it?"

"Because I'm not going to London," she said reluctantly. She looked down at the floor.

"If you're not going there, where are you going?" He looked down at the airline ticket in her hand. She did not try and stop him when he took it from her and examined the contents. He was silent while he read the destination then realisation must have dawned for he said: "Why are you going to Amsterdam? Who do you know there? Wait a minute! No! You can't! Is this where Santana is headed? I'm right, aren't I? You're going after him, aren't you? He's going to Amsterdam to sell the necklace. And you're going to get it back before he does."

She didn't answer for a moment as she tried to think up a good way of telling him. Eventually she said: "What if I am? It's my duty! I found it and I'm going to go and get it back."

"On your own? It's too dangerous."

"I'll be fine."

"No, you won't. The man's sadistic. Have you forgotten what he did to us? He had us buried alive. I'm coming with you."

"No, you're not."

"I am and I'm not arguing with you about it. Wait here."

"Where are you going?"

"I'm going to get a ticket to Schiphol Airport," he replied, smile playing about his lips.

"But what about your passport? It's still back in Alcudia." She was ever practical. He patted his breast pocket.

"Got it here. I never go anywhere without it," he replied, laughing.

She didn't tell him not to come, but instead watched him stride off in the direction of the escalators that would take him down to the KLM desk below. Truth was, she wanted him there, to protect her, to be her shield. The thought of going after Santana, Roberto and the thug alone was scary. She hadn't really thought about the dangers when she'd bought the plane ticket. The hurt and anger caused by Jay had been enough to dampen any fears that may have arisen. Her mind had been caught up by betrayal: Roberto's and Jay's. One a mindless thug, the other lost to another woman or so she had thought. Now she knew Jay was in love with only her and she needn't worry about his love any more, she began to think of what lay ahead and how she would regain the necklace. A creeping awareness of the perils they would face ran through her mind and she shivered. Maybe this wasn't such a good idea, she thought. Was the necklace worth risking her life and that of Jay's again? She looked down at the tatty diary lying on the table and stroked its battered leather cover. Of course, it was, she realised. If she didn't go now, she would never see the necklace again, never finish Harper's great work, would never prove to the world that the lost treasure of Aelia had existed. She stood, picked up the diary and slotted it into her satchel. Time to get started, she resolved and followed Jay downstairs.

 He didn't have any baggage with him, so it was only Nina who had to place her suitcase through check-in. Once that was done they made their way to the departures lounge. Nina was beginning to feel tired and was relieved when their flight was finally called. Here we go, she thought as they boarded.

Turbulence was the only thing that interrupted what was an otherwise boring and uneventful flight, but that didn't bother Nina. She was now more concerned about finding a hotel room for the night and what that might mean. Her stomach did back-flips as she realised tonight would be her first real night with Jay and she cursed herself for not putting on her best underwear. In saying that, Jay would probably have her knickers off before she had even noticed. She turned around to look at him. He had not been able to get a seat beside her and was wedged in the back of the plane between a noisy Dutch family and a young hip couple. He sat impassively for the entire flight, borrowed headphones glued firmly to his ears, ignoring the melee surrounding him. He winked and smiled at Nina. She smiled back, her heart happy and light. She didn't know what she was getting herself into with Jay Reynolds, but it was sure to be an interesting experience. Maybe they wouldn't sleep together. Maybe he was an old-fashioned boy who would wait for her. One last glance at Jay as they disembarked and Nina knew the answer to the latter question. He winked at her and grinned, sending her head spinning. Oh my God! She was having sex tonight, of that she had no doubt.

They disembarked separately and she caught up with him at Customs, dragging her case behind her.

"Um...what are we doing about sleeping arrangements tonight?" she murmured, conscious of the people around them. "I thought we might try to book into one of the airport hotels. What do you think?"

"Sounds good to me," he replied. He took her case off her. "Let me."

"Thanks." She felt awkward. "Do you think we should get single rooms or a double? Double might be cheaper."

He stopped dead in his tracks, face bemused.

"Miss Esposito, are you suggesting what I think you're suggesting?" he asked, pretending shock.

"Well I....."

"Are trying to take advantage of an innocent little thing like me?" A hand was held to his chest as he camped it up.

She laughed. "Absolutely," she said. She poked him in the chest. "Saddle up, Mr Reynolds. You're in for the night of your life!"

"I'm looking forward to it," he grinned.

The SAS Radisson Schiphol was the only hotel close to the airport that had any rooms, the Tourist Information clerk told them. Did they want to book it? They both nodded. Twin or double. Double, they said grinning. No problem, the clerk said. She told them to meet the hotel courtesy bus outside the airport at bus stop 29, just out of the front doors and over to the right. Nina and Jay thanked the woman, gathered up Nina's suitcase and walked hand-in-hand to the door. Nina, heart suddenly in her mouth, was feeling unsure and began to lag behind. Jay gave her hand a quick squeeze.

"You okay?" he asked; his blue eyes full of concern.

"Yes." No. I don't know.

"Sure?"

What was she afraid of? She gave herself a mental kick. This was Jay and she loved him and he loved her. She was sure of it.

"Yes," she replied and meant it.

The hotel was less than a ten-minute drive from the airport. Jay took the lead on booking them in, allowing Nina the opportunity to sink gratefully into a large leather sofa in the reception area. She was exhausted and desperately needed a bath and a lie-down. Before she had time to get comfortable, Jay was back over waggling a plastic key fob in her face. He put her hand out to her and she took it.

"C'mon lazy," he said. "We're on the fifth floor."

Nina followed Jay silently to the lifts. She felt really tired and her legs were like clay. She could barely walk another step.

"Nina, you look exhausted," Jay said.

"Just need to sit down for five minutes," she replied.

"Won't be long now," he said.

The lift came to a stop on the fifth floor and opened to reveal the stylish corridors leading to the rooms. Jay identified the direction of their room and half dragged the sleepy Nina towards it. A few minutes later, their room was found and she was finally able to flop on top of the double bed.

"Fantastic," she murmured.

"Don't get too comfortable," he said scooting over to lie with her, his eyes dark with desire. He gently kissed her neck sending Nina into ecstasy.

"Why?" she murmured, letting the waves of desire wash over

her. If he didn't take her here and now she would just die from longing.

He chuckled and softly stroked her cheek.

"Because…" he breathed in her ear, "I am in desperate need…"

"Mmmm?"

"Of some serious…"

"Mmmmm."

"…food."

He paused. Nina's eyes flickered open.

"What?"

He sat up and dragged her up with him.

"Come on, I'm starving and I know this great little restaurant in the red-light district. You'll love it." He got to his feet. Nina was verging on devastated. He had got her all going and now it had all stopped. Was he bonkers?

"Red light district?" she said, confused. "Weren't we going to just do a little red-light district all of our own here?" she wailed.

"All in good time, my dear," he said pulling her to a sitting position. He kissed her passionately on the lips. "I promise, I will knock the socks off you later."

"You'd better," she muttered. "So why the red-light district?"

"Not what you're thinking," he said. "I know a couple of people down there. They might be able to help you find your necklace. C'mon, get ready. This place stops serving food after nine."

Half an hour later, a shower and a quick change of clothes and Nina was ready to go out again. The hot cleansing water had revived her and she was looking forward to eating out with Jay. He did not have a change of clothes with him, so gave his face a quick wash, brushed his teeth and smoothed his hair.

As good as new, he assured her. She laughed. The room telephone rang and Jay picked it up.

"Hello? Yes, good. We'll be down in five minutes." He replaced the receiver. "Taxi's here."

Nina grabbed her satchel and her jacket. "I'm ready," she replied.

"Great." He grabbed her hand. "Let's go then."

Once in the taxi, Jay instructed the driver to take them to the Sauw Thai Café. Situated, like most places in the city, on the banks of a canal, the Sauw Thai Café didn't look much to Nina from the outside and she was disappointed with the gaudily decorated interior. She frowned as Jay motioned for her to sit down at a wooden table wedged into the smallest corner of the bar. Sparkly red and gold beaded material acted as wall decoration, vying for space with flashy pictures of prophets and gods. The waitresses were young Thai women dressed in slinky evening wear, their long black hair worn down and loose or styled into intricate knots and braids on top of their head. Their make-up was immaculate and their nails beautifully manicured. Nina felt uncomfortably mumsy in her jeans and shirt next to them and played with her hair nervously. Jay leaned over.

"Lady boys," he whispered.

"What? No!" She was shocked. Surely these gorgeous creatures couldn't be men? "Really?" He nodded. "How do you know?"

"It's common knowledge." He grinned. "What are you having? Can I recommend the Red Thai curry with prawns? It's excellent."

A waitress in an aquamarine Mao-collared dress came up to them. She bowed and handed them a menu each.

"What would you like to drink?" she asked in English, her voice low and heavily accented. Nina could hardly take her eyes off this lovely vision before her.

"Erm, just a white wine," she said.

"Dry, medium or sweet?"

"Sweet......I mean dry," she spluttered. She suddenly felt very hot and embarrassed. She could feel Jay's eyes on her.

"I'll have the same," he said. "Oh, and is Jimmy in tonight?"

"I'll go and see," said the waitress.

"Jimmy? Who's Jimmy?" Nina asked.

"A friend of mine. He may just be able to help us."

Within minutes a beaming Asian man appeared carrying two plates stacked with steaming prawns and rice. He placed the plates down on the table before shaking Jay's hand warmly.

"How are you Jimmy?" Jay asked.

"Great, Jay. And you?" Jimmy's eyes twinkled as he took in Nina.

"I've been better," Jay began. "Jimmy let me introduce you to Nina."

"Nina? Nice to meet you," said Jimmy taking Nina's hand and kissing it. "And how do you know Jay?" His words were full of meaning and he winked at the American.

"She's a very good friend of mine," Jay said quickly.

"A good friend? Only a good friend?" Jimmy asked.

"Well...I..." began Nina.

"No, she's my girlfriend," Jay replied and smiled at a surprised Nina. Then before the café owner could say anything else, he added: "Have you got time for a quick chat?"

The man hesitated. "Not really," he said. "It's busy through the back." To Nina he explained: "Everyone comes to the Sauw Thai Café. They can't get enough of Jimmy's great cooking." Back to Jay: "Tell you what, I've got a break around 9.30pm. Will you still be here?"

"Sure," Jay replied.

Jimmy winked, wished them a hearty meal and disappeared into the back, leaving Nina and Jay to enjoy the food. Nina took a mouthful of hers and sat back, a beatific smile on her face as she reveled in the spicy flavours.

"Good?" Jay asked.

"Fantastic," she replied. "How did you find this place?"

"Oh, I've been around." He grinned. "It was recommended to me by a friend some years ago and I make sure I come here every time I'm in Amsterdam. You can't get better Thai food."

Nina tucked into her meal greedily. She couldn't believe how hungry she was. This was just delicious. Over dinner, she chatted amiably about her life; renting an apartment in London with her friend Grace, working for the British Museum and how she became interested in hunting for artefacts and dead people. She told him of her happy upbringing in Scotland and the death of her beloved father, and how her mother had pushed her to be the woman she was today. She spoke of her dreams of one day setting up her own business as a consultant archaeologist, very much as Jay had done. Jay was more guarded about his life, revealing only that although they had originally come from Texas, his family were now in different states. He had a sister in New York and his parents lived on a smallholding in Virginia. Despite Nina's gentle probing, he would talk no more about his private life, preferring to steer the conversation around to her and her half-Spanish, half-English upbringing.

"So that's it?" she asked. "You're telling me nothing more about your life."

"Well, it's so boring. What do you want to know?" He looked uncomfortable.

"Well, where did you go to school? Which university did you study at? How did you come into archaeology?" she began. "How many women have you dated? Were you ever married? What about children?"

He flinched, a reaction that was not missed on her. Had she hit a raw nerve? He did not answer, but looked around the café's and its motley crew of drunken beer-bellied customers coyly smiling waitresses. He leaned across the table.

"Do you think the waitresses sleep with the customers for money?" he whispered, nodding towards a red-faced, sweating drinker feel the leg of one of the bar staff.

"You didn't answer any of my questions," Nina said.

"That's because I didn't want to," he retorted. He glanced at her then looked away.

"Why not?" she asked, "Is there some big bad secret you're hiding?"

"No, it's just that…" He was interrupted by Jimmy beckoning him from the back. "Look, I need to go and speak to Jimmy. I'll be back soon. Order us another couple of drinks, will you?"

Nina watched as he slipped into the back. She wondered about him and what it was he was hiding. What if he really was married? What if he had a child or children? She hadn't given that any thought before, but now it was essential she knew. She had planned to sleep with him tonight, but not if he wouldn't tell her why he was so bugged by her questions. She would talk to him about it when he returned. Jay was away less than half an hour, but it seemed like a lifetime to Nina. She ordered more drinks but grew restless waiting alone at the table and spent the time watching the waitresses flirt and giggle with their clients. They only threw scowls in her direction. When Jay returned, it was to a relieved Nina.

"Thank God," she said. "I thought you had gotten lost or something."

"Jimmy had a few things he wanted to tell me." He did not sit down. Instead, picked up his glass of wine and swigged it. "C'mon," he said holding out his hand for her.

"Where are we going?" "Back to the hotel. I think I know where the necklace is. I'll tell you about it on the way."

The streets were full of gangs of rowdy drunken men on stag nights and wide-eyed women visiting out of voyeuristic fascination. Nina ignored the melee and hurried to keep up with Jay's confident stride. He told her Jimmy had heard from a contact that someone was trying to sell off jewels to the highest bidder. A private auction was to take place at a house in the city's west-end in two days' time. The house was owned by an associate of Santana's and the invitation list featured a whole host of Europe's finest lowlife.

"We must get the police," Nina said.

"And what could they do? It's a private function and the people who are organising it aren't the type who would own up to having anything stolen in their possession," Jay replied. "They'll get out before the police even arrive and then we'll have lost it forever."

"Then we've got to go and get it tonight," she said.

"Santana's yacht won't have arrived at here yet. We'd be better waiting until tomorrow, formulate a plan properly. Besides," he said giving her a sly grin. "I've got other plans for you tonight."

"And can we trust Jimmy not to tell anyone we're here?" she said, ignoring the innuendo.

"Yeah, Jimmy's great. He's real reliable." He took her hand and kissed it. "Shall we get a cab back?"

They picked a taxi up at Centraal Station and relaxed as it wound its way through the streets of Amsterdam in the direction of their hotel. Nina wasn't in the mood for talking much. She felt sleepy and warm and safe. Besides, she didn't want to raise the subject of Jay's suspected 'big secret' right now. She was too comfortable lying here, in his arms. She closed her eyes and nuzzled in. He smelled faintly of aftershave. She must have fallen asleep because the next thing she knew Jay was gently shaking her.

"Wake up sleepy head," he said. "C'mon we're here."

Nina got out of the cab and walked into the hotel. It was a cold night and she shivered as she pushed open one of the doors leading to reception. Its light felt harsh after the cosy darkness of the taxi. As Nina became more awake, she remembered what Jay had planned for them and all the questions she still had to ask before she could succumb to his charms.

"You okay?" he asked wrapping an arm around her as they got into a lift.

"Yes, just tired," she replied cuddling in. Then: "Jay?"

"Yeah?"

"You know what we were talking about earlier?"

"Hmmm?"

"Well, you never really answered my question."

"About what?"

"About whether or not you've been married or had kids," she said quietly. She waited anxiously for the answer.

He chuckled quietly to himself.

"What if I have been married or have kids? What would you do about it?"

"I wouldn't do anything. But it would be nice to know," she muttered.

Jay turned to look at her. His eyes were shining with amusement.

"I have never been married and I don't have any kids," he said.

"So, what's the big secret?" she blurted out.

"Secret?"

"Yes, there was something you weren't telling me in the café!" She was sure of it.

He paused. "I don't have any kids, but..."

Oh God he's sterile or damaged down there or doesn't want kids in the future, Nina stressed.

"My sister and her kids live with me," he said.

Nina sighed with relief.

"That's it? That's all?" she asked breathlessly.

"Yes. She has to live me. She's got no money since her good-for-nothing husband ran off with his secretary! I know, you don't have to say anything, it's such a cliché, but he left her and her boys with huge debts and no way of paying them off. I'm letting her stay with me until she's back on her feet. She keeps house for me , cooks the food, that sort of stuff. It's kinda worked out for both of us."

He was talking, but she wasn't really listening. She was so relieved she had him all to herself.

"Now," he said, suddenly serious. "About you and me..."

"What about you and me?" she asked suddenly very aware of his muscular body leaning against hers. A thrill ran through her as she thought of the night ahead.

"You promised me the night of my life," he murmured as his lips touched her forehead.

"Did I?" she whispered back. The lift doors opened and he pulled her out.

"You know you did," he said as he kissed her.

"And you promised you would knock my socks off," she answered.

"Oh, I'll be doing more than that," he murmured as his hand slipped under her blouse.

Chapter 13

NINA fumbled with the fob to open their door. Her hands were trembling with excitement and trepidation.

"Stupid plastic key thing," she muttered, "what happened to good old-fashioned metal keys that turned a lock?"

"Here, give it to me," said Jay, his blue eyes full of merriment. He slid the plastic card into the lock, there was a click, he pushed the handle down and the door slid open. "See what happens when a woman does a man's job?" he joked.

"Oh, you're gonna pay for that!" replied Nina smiling.

"Yeah?" he grinned then he grabbed her by the waist and swung her into the room. "You're all mine tonight Nina Esposito and nothing is going to interrupt us this time!"

He pulled her close and in the dimness of the room, Nina could see the passion in his eyes. He bent down and kissed her hard on the mouth. Nina could feel her whole body responding to his embrace; her skin was alive to his touch, her blood soared and she could feel the thrill of his kisses slide down her body to the deepest part of her sex. Her lips tingled as the tip of his tongue slid into her mouth. She moaned softly and closed her eyes. Could I be any closer to heaven? She thought as he gently pushed her towards the double bed. Nina felt the bed at the back of her legs and she sat down.

"Stay there," Jay ordered.

"Where are you going?" she asked. Was that it?

"I'm just going to switch the lamps on," he said flicking a switch on the wall. "You're gorgeous Nina and I want to see every part of you."

She blushed and he went to her. Sitting down on the bed beside her, Jay cupped her chin with one hand and kissed her again. His hand slid to her shirt and began to fumble with her buttons. With a flick of his fingers, the buttons popped open exposing her white lacy bra. Using both hands, he pulled the shirt from her trousers and slid it off her shoulders. Still kissing her he went to her belt buckle and the fly of her jeans. She trembled as his fingers skimmed her bare skin. He gently pulled the waistband of her jeans until it was sitting just on her hips.

"Stand up," he whispered.

She stood and he pulled her jeans off, helping her out of them. There was a mixture of delight and desire in his face as he surveyed her.

"You're beautiful," he said as his hands skimmed her hips. "Lie on the bed."

As she lay back, Jay relieved himself of his own clothes, throwing them on the floor before climbing on top of her kissing her gently on her eyelids, her forehead, her cheeks, her lips. She felt a rush of excitement as she kissed him back and it was all she could do to stop herself from moaning his name. His tongue flickered over the lips and then pushed into her mouth exploring, desiring. His hand gently cupped her cheek before sliding down her body to undo her bra. Another flick of his finger and the bra was unclipped. He slid it off her and threw it on the floor. Then he returned to stroke her soft breasts and tweak her nipples before skimming down her stomach to her thighs. He pushed her legs apart and his fingers sought her panties. She moaned as she felt the rush –

"Oh Natalie…" murmured Jay as he pushed his erection against her.

Nina froze. "WHO?"

"What?" he asked.

"You called me Natalie."

"No, I didn't. I said Nina."

"I know what my own name sounds like. You called me Natalie," she repeated as she shoved him off her.

"I did not," he said bemused.

"Who the hell is Natalie?"

"No-one…come here and let's get back to…" he wiggled his eyebrows comically, but the humour was lost on Nina who felt the desire leech out her body. She pulled her legs up and looked at him over the tops of her knees.

"I said, who's Natalie?"

"No-one, honestly, I don't know a Natalie. If I called you that name, I'm sorry, it was a slip of the tongue. Come back over here," he encouraged, but Nina shook her head.

"I don't want to now," she said, "the moment's lost."

He got up into a sitting position, his erection now losing some of its lustre, and frowned.

"I'm sorry Nina, I really am. I don't know what else to say. I don't know a Natalie. I think it was just a heat of the moment thing."

Nina uncurled her legs and slid them off the side of the bed. "I think I'd like to go to sleep now," she said.

"Sure."

She stood up and padded to the en-suite. Switching on the light, she was almost blinded by its glare as she went inside to brush her teeth. She could hear Jay remonstrating outside and allowed herself a little smile. Just as she had squeezed toothpaste on to her brush, Jay was at the door.

"I'm sorry Nina."

"You've already said that," she mumbled through toothpaste. She did not turn around but watched him in the mirror. He looked anxious.

"I know, but I felt I should say it again."

"Apology accepted," she said between brushing.

"Are we okay?" he asked, worry clouding his eyes. She turned around, removed the toothbrush and gave him a toothpaste-y grin.

"Yes, we're okay," she replied. "I'm just tired and desperately need a good night's sleep. I'll be out in a minute. Go and warm the bed up so we can have a cuddle."

"A cuddle or a cuddle?" he asked emphasising the last word with a hopeful look.

"Just a cuddle," she said.

"What about…you know?" His eyebrows rose and fell in a comic fashion.

"Not tonight Jay. I just don't feel like it now. Maybe tomorrow."

"Okay," he said and retreated.

Nina rinsed and replaced the toothbrush on the side of the sink. She looked at herself in the mirror. Was she over-reacting? She wondered. Well how would he feel if she had called him Roberto? Not too happy, she guessed. She had been so looking forward to this moment, but he had just spoiled it with one simple word. She took a deep breath. Maybe tomorrow will be better, she thought as she turned off the light and went to bed.

Jay was already under the covers propped up against the headboard. He raised his arms to her.

"Come on in for a cuddle," he said.

It was her turn to raise her eyebrows.

"Just a cuddle," he promised.

With a smile she climbed in beside him and put her head on his chest. He held her tight and she could hear his heart beating strongly.

"I am sorry you know," he said again.

"Jay?"

"Yes?"

"Shut up and kiss me."

He bent over and kissed her gently on the lips. It was a chaste, simple action, but one that Nina relished. "Oh, fuck it!" she said throwing her arms around his neck and pulling him towards her. "Take me now Jay. I need you."

He looked puzzled. "But you just said…"

"I know what I said and I've changed my mind," she replied kissing him passionately.

"I don't fucking understand you women," he said pushing his growing member against her legs.

"Makes life more interesting," she replied.

She awoke the next morning like the cat that got the cream. She felt just… yummy. Sated and just, well, delicious. She gazed at the man sharing her bed and smiled. He was lying with his back to her, snoring softly. His mussed-up hair making him look younger than his years. He had been excellent in bed; caring, sexy and hot! He had made her body sing and took her to eye-rolling orgasms again and again. She smiled at the thought of her body arching as wave upon wave of desire broke over her. She had never had a lover like him.

"Nina, stop staring at me," he mumbled.

"How did you know…?"

"I can feel your eyes boring into me."

"Sorry."

"Don't be." He rolled over to face her and his eyes were twinkling.

"You were a surprise in bed last night," he said as he stole a kiss.

"What do you mean?" She didn't know whether or not to be insulted or not.

"I mean I thought I'd bedded a pussycat, but ended up with a tiger," he said grinning. "I should have known… the uptight ones are always the ones that shock you."

"What do you mean 'uptight'? I'm not uptight," she snapped, pulling the sheets back as he tried to peel them off her.

"Well you give a good impression of being so," he said gently pulling the sheets out of her hand and giving her naked body beneath an admiring nod, "although that is a bod that's built for sin!"

"Stop it!" she cried, suddenly feeling embarrassed and exposed. She pulled the covers up. "Stop trying to wind me up. I am not uptight. I'm just choosy as to whom I sleep with, that's all."

"Well I'm glad you chose me," he said putting a hand on her waist and pulling towards him. He felt warm as he kissed her gently on the lips. "Oh, so glad!"

His kisses became more passionate and he wrapped his leg around hers, his member, stiffening with every embrace, pushing against her. She responded only too readily to his caresses and before she knew it, he was on top of her gently pushing her legs aside, positioning himself inside her causing her to moan with pleasure at every thrust.

"Oh Nina Esposito!" he moaned as his thrusting grew faster. "You are so beautiful!"

They came together; two reaching ecstasy as one, sweating as one, loving as one. And when it was over, he collapsed on top of her, exhausted and happy, kissing her face and whispering words of love.

They remained entwined for some time each lost in their own thoughts. Then Nina's stomach rumbled and they laughed.

"Well," said Jay gently removing himself, "I guess it's time for breakfast."

He stood up and strode towards the toilet.

"What do you fancy eating this morning?" he asked. "Apart from me, that is!" he added with a wicked twinkle in his eye.

"Don't be so crude," she said, amused. "I don't care what I eat just so long as I eat."

"Cool. Let's get ready and we'll hit the town. We've got a couple of days before I think Santana will get here, so we can take our time. Even enjoy a little holiday whilst we wait."

"Are we looking for a needle in a haystack?" she asked as she got up and followed him into the bathroom. She watched as he turned on the shower and got into the warm water. "Yep."

"It's going to take a miracle to find him isn't it?"

"Yep." The water splashed on his face.

She was silent, downcast. He pulled the shower curtain back and grinned.

"Don't worry, Nina, honey, I have a few contacts here who will keep an eye out for him. Jimmy's on the case. He knows a lot of people and he owes me a favour. When Santana arrives, Jimmy will know and he'll let me know. We'll find him, I promise."

"Okay," she replied buoyed a little by his reassurances.

He stared at her, water running in little rivers down his toned, naked body.

"What?" she asked.

"Are you getting in here with me or what?" he demanded. She didn't need a second invitation.

Nina spent the next couple of days in happy bliss touring Amsterdam with her handsome American boyfriend. Boyfriend? That word sounded so silly, so childish. Was he her boyfriend? He was her lover? She had no doubt about that, but was he her Boyfriend; her partner, her love? She was still unsure. He told her he loved her often enough, but then again so had Roberto all those years ago and look how that turned out. Roberto. The thought of him made her stomach lurch and reminded her of the reason she was here. The necklace! She was going to get the necklace back and return it to the people of Mallorca. Then she and Jay would live happily ever after. If only life were that simple, she thought and felt depressed. Looking at Jay, that beautiful and intelligent man, Nina suddenly realised the full truth of their relationship. How could a man like him love her? He was the darling of archaeology world; well-known and respected across the globe. And she was an insignificant woman from Scotland. Would their story really have a happily ever after? Or was this just another love affair doomed to end as soon as it had begun? She must have sighed out loud for she felt Jay squeeze her hand.

"You okay?" he asked, bright blue eyes full of concern. She

managed a weak smile. They were walking to a small art gallery in the outskirts of the city centre. It was still early and the streets were mercifully quiet of tourists.

"I was just wondering if we will ever get the necklace back," she said.

"Of course, we will. I'll make sure of it!" he replied.

Just at that, Jay's mobile phone rang. He slipped it out of his pocket and looked at the caller ID.

"Jimmy!" he said pressing the button to answer. "Hello? How are you? Yes…u-huh. This morning? Any idea where he might be headed? Are you sure? Great! Thanks buddy. I owe you one!"

He shut the call off and turned to an expectant Nina.

"Game on," he said.

Chapter 14

SANTANA'S yacht had docked at Scheveningen in the early hours of that morning according to Jimmy's source.

"His will be the biggest boat in the harbour, but nobody'll think twice about it being there. The place gets loads of different folks turning up at all times of the year," Jay told Nina.

"He'll head straight for Amsterdam," Nina mused. They were hurrying to Canal Strasse. "Why are we going back here?" she asked as they turned the corner towards the Sauw Thai Café.

"For coffee," Jay replied, "and to wait for Jimmy's sources to find out where Santana and that your old boyfriend turn up. Jimmy's got a fair idea of where he might be going but wants to be sure."

Jimmy was polishing glasses and having a heated conversation in Dutch with a man on a red leatherette bar stool. About what Nina did not know. As soon as he saw her handsome companion, Jimmy broke off and gave Jay a wide grin.

"Jay my friend, how are you? Nice to see you and your lady friend again. Please sit," he said waving them to a booth, "and have some wine with me."

Jay shook his head.

"It's a bit early in the day for me, Jimmy." He sat with his back to the bar, facing the entrance. Nina sat opposite.

"What can I get you?" the older man said, giving Nina an approving look.

Jay got straight down to business. "Have you heard anything?" Jimmy gave him a warning look and nodded almost imperceptibly to the man sitting at the bar. He slipped into the booth beside them and said in a whisper: "Keep it down. Santana has eyes and ears everywhere. That man over there– he's one of them. I've been asking a few questions about his business, but he's keeping everything close to his chest. He did say he was expecting a big fish in today." He stood up and said loudly:

"So, what brings you to Amsterdam, my friend? Are you buying or selling this time?" He raised his eyebrows and looked pointedly at Jay. The American picked up the cue.

"Buying," Jay replied carefully. "I'm looking for some gems for a wealthy client who's not too particular about where they came from. He wants to use them to create something stunning for his new young wife. Apparently, she's into designing her own jewellery. Having seen some of the things she's had made, I would say she should think about changing careers, but who am I to say anything? So long as her husband pays me and pays me well, I don't care."

Nina watched and listened to this little act with interest. She glanced at the man at the bar and couldn't make out if he was listening or not. Was Jay honestly hoping he would fall for this? She rolled her eyes and decided to stay out of it. Jay continued: "You wouldn't happen to know if anyone's selling anything good at the moment?"

Jimmy shook his head and sucked on his bottom lip.

"Nothing like that," he said almost a little too sorrowfully, "but if I hear of anything I will be sure to let you know."

"Thanks. I knew I could count on you."

Just then, one of Jimmy's chefs stuck his head out of the kitchen and said something to him in Thai.

"Excuse me please," Jimmy said. "I have to go and deal with this."

Nina looked at Jay, amusement playing about her eyes. Jay responded with a shrug and a look that said: well, anything's worth a try.

"What are our plans for this morning?" she asked in a quiet voice.

He leaned over the table, gave her a peck on the lips and whispered: "Let's stay here a little while and see what happens. I think our friend at the bar may yet lead us to where we want to go."

"How?" she mouthed.

"Darling," Jay said a little louder than normal, "do you think you could postpone your shopping trip this morning? I need to see a few associates about that damned jewellery and I think your eye would be an asset. You can at least tell me what you think the client's wife may like."

He gave her a look that told her to play along.

She returned with a loud sigh.

"Fine!" she said, "so long as you buy me something too!"

She threw Jay a pout for good measure and was surprised by his startled reaction.

"Anything for you!" he said and gave her the kind of look that would melt the polar ice-caps. Nina felt a flutter go through her stomach and into her throat. She swallowed hard and managed a smile. Wow he was sexy when he was acting.

"Good," she said. "I could do with some new jewellery."

"You could also do with a good spanking for being so cheeky," he murmured, eyes never leaving hers, "but that can wait 'til later."

Nina suddenly felt a little hot under the collar. She heard Jay chuckle softly at her discomfort. She was about to retort when a Euro pop song seared the air. She looked over to the bar and saw the stranger pick up his phone. The music died and he answered in English.

"Yah, yah, today? Now? Where? Okay see you then." He disconnected and slipped the phone into his pocket. He proceeded to jot something down on a beer mat. Downing his beer and wiping his mouth with the back of his hand, he got up and shouted his goodbyes to Jimmy through the kitchen door. There was a muffled reply. The man smiled before taking the beer mat over to the booth where Nina and Jay were sitting.

"Ah Jimmy's friend, yes?" he said in a thick Dutch accent. Jay nodded. "I heard you talk of jewellery. If you are looking for something nice, try this man." He placed the mat on the table and with a curt nod, left.

Jay whipped up the mat and studied it carefully.

"What does it say?" Nina wanted to know. She stood up and gathered her things.

"It's an address a few streets away. I think I know that place," said Jay. "Where are you going? To the address?"

"No," she said with a smile, "we can do that later. I'm going to see where that man is going. I think he's a much better bet."

Jay threw a few Euros on the table and bolted out after Nina who was already hurrying down the street. She had seen the man disappear around the next corner and slowed as she reached it. Cautiously peering round, she saw him stride towards a little café. Without looking around, the man ducked inside. Nina slowed her pace and stepped into the doorway of an empty shop. She stood there for some moments when a hand on her shoulder made her jump. She squeaked in surprise and turned around to find Jay at her back.

"Why didn't you wait for me?"

"I would have lost him," she said.

"Where is he now?"

"In the…oops, there he is, get back!"

They both flattened themselves in the doorway. A few seconds passed and then Nina peered round.

"He's not seen us," she said with relief. "Come on."

Jay sighed and followed as she ran down the street. She slowed again at the bottom, cautiously looking around the corner to see where the man went next. As she watched, he approached the bright red door of a canal house and lifted the ornate gold door knocker. Some moments passed before the door was opened by a middle-aged man in an expensive-looking suit. They exchanged a few words before the man from the bar was taken inside. The other man took a quick look up and down the street before going inside and shutting the door. Nina made to move, but Jay's hand on her shoulder prevented her. He gently pulled her back to the corner just as a large black limousine pulled up at the house. A chauffeur in a charcoal grey uniform and cap got out and opened the rear door. Nina gasped. "Roberto!" Then another, smaller, man in an immaculate pale linen suit emerged carrying a little leather case.

"Santana!" Jay whispered.

"And it looks like he's got what we're looking for."

They watched as Roberto stood aside to allow Santana to approach the door first, but it was Roberto who knocked. It was answered by the same man who opened it before. He welcomed the pair like old friends, shaking their hands vigorously and slapping Roberto on the back. Nina and Jay watched them all disappear inside.

"Bingo!" said Nina triumphantly.

"Don't count your chickens yet," Jay warned. "We've still to get the necklace."

"Yes, but at least we know where it is now."

Nina made to move, but Jay yanked her back again. "What do you think you're doing?" he snapped, blue eyes blazing.

"I'm going to confront them," she hissed.

"Like hell you are."

"Well, have you got a better idea?"

"Yeah, we're going to sit it out," he replied pointing a little Brown café nestled behind the stalls of a Dutch cheese market. "We'll get a good view from there without being noticed."

"But…!"

"No buts!" he said putting his arm around her waist. "Let's go and I don't want to hear another word."

Ignoring her feeble protestations, Jay manoeuvred Nina through the brightly-coloured stalls laden with huge rounds of cheese, over to the café where he finally let her go. He pointed to a table at the window where he expected her to sit. Nina, taken aback at this show of masculinity, could only slide herself on to a wooden chair and watch whilst he went to the bar. He ordered and as he was counting his money, the barman took out a book and offered it to Jay. He shook his head. He didn't want drugs.

Minutes later he was sitting next to her. He smiled.

"I ordered you a tea," he said.

"Maybe I didn't want a tea," she replied.

"And maybe you will get that spanking after all," he promised, eyes twinkling mischievously.

Nina's stomach did a flip. She could feel her face burning.

"Stop teasing me!" she pleaded as the barman brought over two cups of tea.

"You love it!" her companion promised.

"Why didn't you let me go to the door," Nina asked after a little while. She stared over to the house that held her necklace. Through the forest of market stalls, she could just make out the door and was worried that they would miss something important stuck as they were inside the café.

"It's too risky. We don't know who's in there and whether they are armed or not. People like Santana would have no qualms about making us disappear. He might deny it, but he tried before remember?"

How could Nina forget being imprisoned in that cold tomb? She shivered at the recollection.

"Let's give it a while," her companion said, "and see what happens."

Two hours passed very slowly and only five people entered the house: a grey-haired man in a pinstripe suit and his bejewelled young lady friend; a small ferret-like man in Chinos and a white shirt; and an elegant older woman in furs trailed by her chauffeur carrying a small lap dog. Nina tapped her foot impatiently. She had drunk three cups of tea and eaten one pastry and she was getting fed up waiting around.

"Why don't we…?" she began.

"No. We wait." Jay cut her off.

"But…"

"Nina, it's too dangerous. Something will happen soon, I know it," he promised.

Another hour passed and Nina could take no more. She

waited until Jay went to the toilet before paying the bill and skipping out the door. Before she could think things through, she wove through the stalls and strode confidently up to the red door. Heart beating madly, mouth dry with nerves, but determined, she reached for the door knocker. It was a beautifully crafted in the shape of a pineapple. She felt its cold metal under her hand and with another deep breath for courage gave the door a knock. As she waited for an answer she glanced back at the café to see a furious-looking Jay emerge into the square. With a face like thunder, he ran through the market, coming to get her.

Behind her, someone said something in Dutch.

She turned to see the familiar face of the doorman. She gave him her best smile.

"Good morning," she said.

"It's not morning," said the man in a heavily accented English, "I think you'll find it's now the afternoon."

"Ah, yes, I meant good afternoon…er…" she glanced around to see Jay was now crossing the road, his face set in a deep frown. "Is…er…I mean…"

"What can I help you with madam?" the man asked with strained politeness.

"I'm here to see Mr Santana," she said quickly. Jay was nearly on her.

"Do you have an appointment?"

"Er…"

"Yes, we have an appointment," Jay interrupted.

"May I have your names?" said the man.

"That won't be necessary," replied Jay pushing past him with Nina following close behind.

"We're old friends," she added sweetly.

"Sir! Madam! You cannot go up there! I insist!"

Jay and Nina hurried to the ornate wooden staircase. Filtering down from above were the unmistakable sounds of partying. They ran up to the first floor where a man was standing with his back to them. He turned around and was startled.

"What are you doing here?" Roberto snarled.

Nina did not hesitate. She threw a punch at him, sending him sprawling.

"You dirty, two-faced, scheming bastard!" she yelled. "We could have died down there! You left us to die! How could you?"

"I was following orders!" Roberto gasped. "Jay! A bit of help here!"

"You're asking for my help after what you did to us? That's rich!" Jay replied. "I could stand here and let her beat you to death," he continued, "but I'll save that for later!" He grabbed a furious Nina by the waist and pulled her away.

"I should tear you apart limb from limb!" she screeched as Roberto, shaken by her attack, attempted to tidy himself up. "You bastard!"

"Miss Esposito, please show a little decorum whilst you are in the house of my friend," a familiar voice said.

Nina and Jay turned around to come face to face with a smiling Santana. He held a full crystal brandy glass in one hand and a large Cuban cigar in the other. Drawing on it he surveyed the scene. Unlike his underling, Santana showed no sign of shock at them being here.

"So, you've caught up with me," he said with a sly smile. "I thought I had gotten rid of you two for good. My friend over there assured me you were taken care of, but I see he did not do a good job. Never mind, it doesn't matter now." He was staring at Nina as he said this and his leer made her feel very uncomfortable. "You really are an attractive woman, Miss Esposito especially when you're roused."

"That's Dr Esposito to you," she snapped.

"Feisty too. I like that in a woman. Makes bedding them all the more fun," he chuckled and blew a smoke ring in her direction.

Nina shuddered, but Santana did not seem to see.

"I've come for the necklace. The people of Mallorca deserve to keep their heritage, not have it stolen by someone like you!" she growled.

Santana surveyed her for a moment, that sly smile still playing about his lips. Then he turned to go back inside a nearby doorway.

"This might come as a surprise to you, Dr Esposito, but I like you. So, I'll make a bargain with you." He walked into the other room. With a nod of he indicated Jay and Nina to follow. They entered a large reception room filled with richly dressed people and waiters serving drinks on silver trays. They as one turned to look at them. Santana came to a stop at a table where he put down his drink. He turned to face Nina.

"I'll give you back the necklace if you promise to stop harassing me. Much as I'd like to… accommodate you Doctor Esposito, I'm starting to get a little tired of you. Pity."

Nina stared at him in disbelief. Had she heard correctly? Annoyed at her silence, Santana said again, this time more forcefully: "I said I'll give you back the necklace if…"

"Yes, I heard you the first time," she replied, "Just get to the catch."

"Oh!" replied the businessman with a wink to his audience. "There is no catch." There was a murmuring of laughter in the room, which Nina could only scowl at. She looked at Jay who was looking as puzzled as she felt.

"Okay, fine," she said holding out a hand. "I want it back now."

With a smirk, Santana reached into his suit pocket and pulled out the golden necklace. He threw it at Nina who caught it in one hand. She held it up to the light. It glittered enticingly. She smiled.

"I'd say thanks," she said as a parting shot, "but you stole it from me in the first place."

She turned to Jay and they were about to go when Santana spoke again.

"Oh, Miss Esposito, I'd have those jewels looked at by an expert if I were you… before you go public with your find," he said.

Nina looked at the jewels in her hand and with a frown, turned.

"What do you mean?"

"Well, you know how it goes" said the man with a smirk and shrug, "when so many people are searching for the same treasure, chances are someone else got there first…"

"Grave robbers?" Nina muttered.

"My man looked at the necklace and he seemed to think it's nothing but a worthless glass copy." He gave her a patronising pat on the arm. "Goodbye my dear. I hope our paths never cross again."

"Nina, come on, let's get out of here," Jay said pulling her towards the door.

"I think that would be a very good idea!" Nina heard Santana say as she was hurried down the stairs.

"But Jay!"

"You've got the necklace. We are still alive. Let's go. I know a man who knows a man who can look at the necklace. He's the best in the business. He'll be able to tell us the truth or not."

Nina nodded meekly. Surely her necklace was not a fake?

Chapter 15

"YES, it's a fake. Those 'jewels' are indeed just glass replicas. Good ones, but fakes nonetheless," the jeweller said in perfect English. "The chain itself is original though."

Nina felt the bottom drop out of her world. No, it can't be true!

"The Romans couldn't have made such fine replicas," she whined.

"No, they didn't, but someone closer to our own time did. I would say these are no more than…" Here the man took a deep breath whilst he made his best guess. "Hmmm… five years old."

"That means someone got to the necklace before us," Jay said. "But who?"

"Why would they take all the trouble to swap the stones? They would have to steal the necklace, commission someone to create the new stones and then replace the necklace on the body. It doesn't make sense," Nina said. She flopped into the nearest chair and rubbed her face with her hands. She suddenly felt exhausted. "Why go to all that trouble?"

"I don't know," he replied. He seemed just as devastated as she was. "Come on, let's go back to the hotel and try to figure this out." He held out his hand and she took it, allowing herself to be pulled to her feet. Jay thanked the jeweller and gave him some Euros for his trouble. The pair then made their way back to the hotel, the fake jewels carefully placed in Nina's bag.

The hotel room was hot and stuffy, being so fine outside, so Nina opened a window to let in some fresh air and then sat down on the double bed. She felt like crying. She had fought all the way to find this necklace of legend only to find out someone had got there before her and had swapped it for a fake. If it had been ordinary grave robbers, she could understand, but the fact that someone took all the trouble to replace the jewels was perplexing. Why go to all that trouble and expense? She couldn't fathom it. Whilst Jay telephoned Room Service for some toasted sandwiches and coffee, Nina slipped Joseph Harper's diary from her bag.

"What's that?" Jay wanted to know.

"Joseph Harper's diary of his last expedition to find Aelia and her necklace. I thought there might be something I've missed."

"Can I see it?" Jay asked holding out a hand. Nina passed it over and watched as he flicked through.

"There are pages missing at the end."

"I know."

"Why would someone remove them?" he wondered. "Rework? Mistakes? Or... was there some great secret hidden in the last pages?"

"That's another mystery," she shrugged.

And then it dawned on them both at the same time.

"He found it!" Nina said it before Jay could. "He found the tomb and Aelia and the necklace. He found it and he wrote about it in this diary." She held it up.

"So, he wrote about finding the necklace and then what?" Jay replied eyes shining, "Who tore the pages out? Harper himself or someone else?"

Nina was quiet for a moment.

"Let's say he found the necklace. He went into the tomb, removed the necklace and then… no, that still doesn't make sense. Why would he take the real necklace and then replace it with a fake? Joseph Harper was made a laughing stock in his later years because of his obsession with Aelia. If he had found it, surely he would have told the world about it? Then he would have had his reputation restored."

"Shame he's not around anymore to answer these questions," Jay said going to the door to the Room Service waiter.

"His wife and son are!" Nina replied excitedly, "and I know just where to find them. Pass me the phone, will you?"

"What are you doing now?"

"I'm phoning the airport to see if we can get on the next plane to London. We're going to see Mrs Harper and her son and see what they know. We owe it to the people of Mallorca to find their jewels. We owe it to Aelia."

"Isn't that a bit melodramatic for this time in the day?" Jay joked. "It's only lunchtime."

"Maybe," said Nina, annoyed, "but I mean every word of it!"

Landing in London at 10 o'clock that night, Nina wasted no time in taking Jay back to the flat she shared with Gracie, only stopping for some late-night fish 'n' chips en-route. Her flatmate, dressed in a pair of men's pyjamas and furry monster slippers seemed more than happy to see Jay walk through the door.

"Well you're a sight for sore eyes," she crooned as Nina introduced the American. "Here's me expecting to spend Sunday night all on me lonesome and you two come waltzing in the door with chips! Go on give us some and I promise I will let you have snogging rights to the sofa."

"Snogging rights?" Jay asked Nina bemused.

"I'll explain later," she said blushing and quickly offering Gracie some chips in the hope that it would shut her up. "Anything been happening while I was away?"

"Not much," Grace replied. Then she remembered something. "Oh yeah that boss of yours. George is it? Was looking for you. He said he needed to speak to you about your extended holiday? Does that make sense?" Nina nodded. "Anyway," Gracie added suddenly coming on all coy, "I can see three's a crowd, so I'll just leave you two lovebirds alone and go get my beauty sleep."

"Goodnight Gracie," Nina said giving her a smile. Gracie danced over to the door and there she paused.

"Oh, and can I just add one thing?" she said. "Can you please keep the noise down? My bedroom is only next door and some of us are working tomorrow, you know!"

Before a mortified Nina could answer, a laughing Gracie had disappeared out of the door and closed it shut with a definite click.

"What was all that about?" Jay smiled.

"Just Gracie being Gracie and thinking she's being funny," she explained. She looked at the empty chip wrappers in Jay's hand. "You finished?" He nodded. "Good, come on. Let's go and get some sleep."

"Sleep?" He raised an eyebrow. "Or SLEEP?"

"Jay you are incorrigible!" she gasped. "When I say sleep, I mean sleep. You know, the thing you do when you close your eyes and the next thing you know it's morning?"

"Oh," he replied snaking his arms around her waist and kissing the back of her neck sending shivers down her spine, "I was hoping for a bit more than just plain old sleep."

"You are?" She groaned and turned to face him. He took her into his arms and pulled her into his body for a passionate embrace and close enough for her to feel the erection on her thigh. "Oh, you are! Okay then, come on, but keep it down because…"

"I know: Gracie needs her beauty sleep!" he chuckled.

Standing outside a neat 1930s semi in New Malden in Surrey, Nina hesitated at the gate to the pristine front garden. She suddenly felt afraid to go further.

"Do you think it's too early to call?" she asked Jay who was standing impatiently nearby. They had been there for a good ten minutes and he was beginning to feel fed up.

"Not chickening out, are you?" he asked, a smile playing about his lips. Nina scowled at him.

"No," she replied, "it's just that Mrs Harper will be an old lady now and I don't want to scare her. Joseph Harper was also a big hero of mine and…well…what if I found out he was a big phoney and took the real jewels for himself? I really hero-worshipped him when I was a child. After my dad died, reading about his exciting discoveries and seeing him on the telly made me forget about how much I was missing dad for a little while. What if I go in there and I'm disappointed? What if he was a big fat fraud?"

"It's a chance you're going to have to take, honey," Jay replied slipping his arm around her waist and giving her a squeeze. She smiled and squeezed him back, pleased to have him with her, a strong and solid presence.

There was the sound of a door being wrenched open. They looked up to see an angry looking 40-something man storming out of the Harper house. He was wearing a t-shirt and jeans. On his feet were what Nina thought of as 'dad slippers'. His dark hair was slicked back over his head.

"Hoi! You two!" he yelled. "What are you doing hanging around my mother's house?"

"Oh! Sorry!" Nina gasped, flustered. "We were looking for Mrs Harper, Joseph Harper's widow. Does she live here?"

"What do you want to speak to her about?" the man snarled. His dark eyes were looking at them with pure malice.

"Do you know her? Is this the right address?"

"What's it to you?"

"Now hold on buddy." Jay stepped in unwilling to let the man's rudeness continue. "The lady just asked a question. You could at least answer it in a civil manner."

Before the man could answer, a small shadow was at his back. It emerged from the house in the shape of a little old lady with white hair and more wrinkles than Rip Van Winkle.

"I am Mrs Harper," she announced in a clear voice. "What do you want from me?"

"Mum, I'll handle this," Harper junior said. "They're just here to make fun of dad again. I'll get rid of them."

"Is that true?" the old lady asked.

"No," Nina replied, "in fact, it's quite the opposite. I am a huge fan of your husband's work…he's the reason I became an archaeologist…and well…"

"My father's dead, Miss…?"

"Esposito. Dr Nina Esposito and this is my colleague Dr Jay Reynolds."

The couple nodded to Nina and Jay.

"I know your father has passed on," she said, "but I wondered if I could have a word with both of you about something he had been working on."

"Not today," replied the son. Jack, his name is Jack, Nina thought remembering the diary entries. Then with a curt: "We're not interested. Goodbye," he turned and began to usher his ageing mother inside.

"Not even if it's about Aelia's necklace?" she shouted after them. Mrs Harper hesitated at the front door but was urged on by her son. "I know about the switch!" Nina continued. They turned as one.

Mrs Harper looked at her son and then looked around the neighbourhood, scared someone had heard. She let out a resigned sigh.

"You'd better come in," she said with a worried look.

The Harpers' living room was small and comfortable, and decorated with a 70s retro feel. It was not as light and airy a room as Nina had been used to in Mallorca, and rather duller. A mud-coloured sofa and two armchairs were positioned around a replica gas fire and an ancient telly sat in one corner of the room. There were shelves in the small alcove behind one chair and a couple of photographs of Joseph Harper adorned the fire surround. This was not the home of someone whose wealth had been extracted from the sale of stolen jewels.

"Please take a seat," Mrs Harper told her guests. "I'm just going to put on the kettle. Jack, be a dear and keep them company."

Jack Harper took an armchair and sat silently growling at the two archaeologists whilst the sounds of chinking chinaware filtered through from the kitchen. "I can't believe you're bothering an old lady about that stupid necklace," he said at last, breaking the awkward silence.

"We just want to ask you both a couple of questions," Nina replied.

"I don't think we'll be able to help," he snarled and lapsed back into sullen silence.

The door burst open to the clink of tea things. Mrs Harper thrust forward an old-fashioned tea trolley laden with cups, saucers, milk jug, a large teapot and a plate of plain biscuits.

"Here we are!" she said a little too breezily. "It's been a long time since I've entertained. Does anyone want sugar? I never put any out, I wasn't sure. Most people don't take it nowadays. Of course, Joseph, God bless his soul, was a great lover of sugar in tea. He had three teaspoonfuls in every cup!"

She handed round cups of steaming hot tea, offering the pair milk and a biscuit. Nina refused the former but tucked into a Custard Cream. She hadn't had one since she had been a child.

"So," said Mrs Harper placing her own tea on the mantelpiece and sitting down on the other armchair, "what can we do for you? You said something about a necklace?"

Nina looked at the old woman and noticed for the first time how frail she seemed. She was a small, slim woman, but her eyes fascinated Nina most. Her mother always told her that you could tell a person's character by their eyes and Nina could see a certain steeliness in Mrs Harper's.

"Yes, we wanted to ask you a few questions about the necklace," she said.

"So you've said already," replied Mrs Harper. There was a steeliness in her tone of voice too.

"Did your husband ever find it?"

Mrs Harper picked up her teacup and saucer and took a sip.

The action would have seemed normal to those sitting watching had she not exchanged glances with her son opposite. She sighed.

"My husband found the tomb," she said bitterly. "He was obsessed with finding it and he was obsessed with her."

"Who?" Jay asked sitting forward on his seat.

"That woman, the Roman one!"

"You mean Aelia?" Nina asked.

"Yes her! He even claimed she came to him in his dreams and that he had fallen in love with her. He said she had bewitched him. He was a stupid old fool who drank too much whisky," she muttered.

"So, was it on your holiday to Mallorca in 1979 that he found her tomb?" Nina continued.

"How do you know about that?"

Nina produced the diary from her bag. Mrs Harper frowned.

"I gave that to the British Museum – how did you get it?" she snarled.

Nina pulled out her museum id card and showed it to the Harpers.

"I work there, I'm a doctor of archaeology Mrs Harper and I have a great interest in Aelia's necklace." She paused. "So, did he find it then?"

Mrs Harper pursed her lips and Nina was afraid she would not speak again, but after a few tense moments, the old lady talked.

"No. It was in 1981. He forced us back to that island to look again. Said he had found new evidence that would lead to the tomb. I don't know what it was so don't ask me. So, he went back and he took us with him…" Here she looked regretfully over to Jack. "…and he found the tomb. End of story."

"But it wasn't the end of the story, was it Mrs Harper?" Jay prompted.

The old lady looked sharply at him and let out another sigh. "No, it wasn't," she replied.

"Mum you don't have to say any more," Jack said. "It's too painful."

"No," she said resignedly. "After all these years it will be good to tell someone else." She put down her teacup and sat back in her chair. "As I said my husband was obsessed with that Roman princess or whatever she was. She was like another woman in our marriage. I nearly left him that year because he was so besotted with her. I suppose I could have understood if he had run off with another woman, but to be in love with someone who had been dead a thousand years? That was just too much," she said eyes filling with long unshed tears. "Anyway, he found the tomb and the Roman remains and the necklace, and he removed it intending to bring it home so he could finally put all the nay-sayers to rest... And that's when the trouble really started. The day he found the tomb, he came back to our hotel full of excitement and he showed us the necklace. It was the most beautiful thing I had ever seen. That night, he had terrible nightmares, he couldn't sleep and paced up and down in our room like a man possessed. The next morning, he told me he was going to take it back, she needed it back – those were his words - and seal up the tomb for good. When I asked why, he said she had come to him in a dream and told him to return her jewels. I told him to stop being so stupid, but he wouldn't listen. He took Jack with him. I don't really know what happened in the tomb, but they came back a few hours later covered in mud."

Nina turned to the son. "So, you took the necklace back?"

"Yes," he replied.

"And how did you get into the tomb?"

"Through an old well in the middle of a field," he said.

"And you blocked the entrance back up?"

"Yes. Dad showed me how to do it to make it look like it would have a thousand years ago. He was always teaching me old skills."

Nina nodded her head knowing only too well the job had not been a good one.

"So how did the fake jewels come to be on the body instead of the real ones?" she asked.

"We don't know anything about that!" Jack snapped, but his eyes shifted and Nina knew he was lying. "Isn't that right mum?"

"Oh yes!"

"What did you spend the money on?" Jay asked sharply.

"I don't know what you mean," replied Jack as casually as he could muster. His face had reddened and he was sweating.

"We know you swapped the jewels," he growled.

"You're lying! We never swapped the jewels. Why would we?"

"We got fingerprints from the fakes."

"You're lying." Jack glared at Jay only to be met by the steely stare of a man who knew he was in the right. Jack looked away, pretending concern for his mother.

"Well, let's leave that up to the police to find out," Jay replied getting to his feet. He motioned for Nina to do the same. "I'm sure they'll be interested in jewel theft."

"You have nothing! You're bluffing!" Jack stammered.

"I can assure you Mr Harper, I never bluff."

This time the son could not escape the intensity of Jay's stare and the lesser man stood there like a rabbit caught in headlights. Moments passed before Jay released Jack and turned to the mother.

"Mrs Harper," he began, "do you really want us to take the necklace to the police?"

"No! Please! Don't! I beg you not to!" Mrs Harper wailed. "Don't do that! We didn't think anyone would ever know."

All eyes turned to her.

"Mum, no!" Jack said rushing to her side. "Don't say anything else! They have nothing on us!"

"No son, it's time we came clean." She turned to Nina and Jay. "Sit down and I'll tell you all about it. Yes, we did take it. It was my idea. Jack didn't want to, but we had no choice. I made him do it. That day in 1981 when they were returning the necklace to the tomb, I told him to take the necklace from the body when his dad wasn't looking and hide it in his clothing. I felt we deserved it after all the things Joseph put us through searching for the blasted thing." She sighed. "It nearly ended our marriage and it took Joseph away from his son so I felt that we – Jack and me – deserved some compensation, so we took it. My plan was to leave his father and give Jack the life he deserved.

"So, we took it and I hid it in the house until I could find out how to go about selling the jewels without Joseph knowing. Things improved slightly between us and I decided to stay with Joe for Jack's sake. I won't say it was a very loving marriage, but it was a marriage non-the-less. I kept the necklace hidden for 30 years as a kind of insurance. I had no idea what to do with it, who to go to sell the jewels. Then disaster struck…"

"Your husband became ill?" Nina interrupted.

"Yes, Joseph was diagnosed with lung cancer 12 months ago and given less than a year to live," she continued. "Bloody man insisted on going back to see that skeleton one last time. Said he wanted to tell her he was coming to her soon. He couldn't be talked out of it. He insisted on it. He even booked himself on a flight to Mallorca without us knowing. I don't know how he thought he was going to get there on his own because by that time he was too weak to go anywhere by himself. We only found out when he asked me for his passport.

"So, I had to have the stones copied and had glass replicas put back in the original settings. The three of us flew back to Mallorca before Joe started any treatment and I insisted Jack go with him into the tomb. He made sure he was first in and was able to slip the necklace back on the body before his father could see. We couldn't let him know you see; it would have killed him. I still loved him, despite all the things he had done and said, and I couldn't see him going to his grave broken-hearted that someone had stolen the necklace from his beloved skeleton."

"I don't understand something," Nina said. "Why didn't you just take the original necklace and return that?"

Mrs Harper looked shamefaced. "We had already prised all the jewels out of their settings."

"Why not put them all back?"

"Because we had already sold two and the rest, well, I still feel we deserve them. There was no way I was going to put all those precious stones back in the ground. We needed the money. Joseph had been so obsessed with that Roman woman for so long that he had become a laughing stock. Things got worse over the last ten years. He began drinking heavily and getting into fights. No-one would hire him. We had no money. Then when he became ill and, well, life just got harder. Why shouldn't we get something out of it?" she said bitterly.

"So, if you sold two," Jay said carefully, "where are the others?"

Mrs Harper looked up at her son and he nodded. He stood up and left the room. "What happens now?" she asked.

"I don't know," Nina replied. She hadn't thought any further than quizzing Mrs Harper and her son. "I suppose we will need to speak to the Mallorcan authorities. It'll be up to them."

Jack appeared at the door carrying a shoebox. He handed it to his mother before resuming his seat. Mrs Harper peeled the lid off and handed the box to Nina. The young archaeologist peered inside and gasped: it was filled with sparkling amethysts, exquisite pearls and a large white opal. With a shaking hand, she lifted the opal from the box and held it up to the pale light filtering into the living room. It sparkled and gleamed.

"Wow!" she said mesmerised by its beauty.

"Wow indeed," Mrs Harper said bitterly. A solitary tear slid down her wrinkled cheek and she hastily brushed it away with a trembling hand. "What's going to happen to us? I don't want Jack to be blamed for this because it was all me. He was just a boy."

Nina put the opal back in the box and gave her a sympathetic look.

"I really don't know," she said.

"We only took two little ones," the older woman continued. "We needed the money you see."

"I'm sorry, but it won't be up to me. These gems and the necklace settings will have to be returned to Mallorca," she said. "But, I'll explain what happened: that you only sold the two gems because your husband was ill."

"Thank you," Mrs Harper said gratefully.

Jay stood up. "We'd best get going."

"Goodbye Mrs Harper," Nina said rising to her feet. "Thank you for being so honest with us."

She walked towards the door and then paused. She turned around and took the diary from her back offering it to a horrified Mrs Harper. "Do you want this?"

"No. I don't want to be reminded of that time. Keep it."

"What happened to the last few pages," Nina asked flicking to the back of the journal and showing her where they had been ripped out.

"I don't know what you mean," the old lady replied with a frown. "The diary was complete when Jack took it to the British Museum with all the other stuff we donated. Isn't that right Jack?" Her son nodded. "In fact, we fully expected to hear from the museum once they had read the last pages."

"What did they say?" Nina had to know.

"It was that last expedition. He wrote down how he found the tomb and the body and the necklace. He described everything in great detail, even that he had put the necklace back."

"So, someone ripped the pages out between you donating the diary and me getting it, but who?" Nina wondered aloud.

"Who did you give it to?" she asked.

Mrs Harper looked at Jack who was already trying to remember.

"I think it was a man called George. I can't remember his surname, but it was definitely George. Nice man," he said.

"George Rayburn?" she asked.

"Yes, that's it. Rayburn. That's the name. Why? Do you know him?"

"He's my boss."

"I'll kill him!" Nina snarled as she and Jay left the Harper house with the shoebox of jewels. "He ripped out those pages to stop me finding the tomb."

"Don't be silly Nina. Why would he do that?" Jay said soothingly.

"I'm going to find out!"

"What? Where are you going?"

"To see George to ask him why he did it."

"You don't know he did anything. You just can't march up to the man and accuse him."

"Watch me!" she said fiercely and Jay knew better than to argue.

Chapter 16

"WHY did you do it George? I trusted you. You know how much this meant to me! I thought you were my friend!" Nina shouted as she flew into her boss's office and planted her palms on his desk. George looked at Nina like she had just flown down from Mars, then regained his composure, and cleared his throat before speaking.

"And hello to you too Nina," he replied casually, but the shock in his eyes belied his apparent composure. "I'm fine, how are you?"

"Not fine, George. Not fine at all. How could you?"

"What are you talking about?" The colour was starting to return to his face, but he still looked out of his depth.

"This!" she blazed and threw Joseph Harper's diary down in front of him. George took it up and flicked through the pages. "Open it at the end," Nina ordered.

"I don't understand…"

"Just do it."

He turned to the back where the pages had been ripped out.

"How many are missing?" Nina demanded.

"How should I know?"

"Did you destroy them? Hide them?"

"Nina, have you gone crazy?" replied her boss. "I really don't know what you're talking about. How would I know about the ripped-out pages? The last time I saw this you had it and were waving it about in my face."

"You collected the Joseph Harper archive from his widow. I know that you personally catalogued and stored everything in it. The Harpers say the diary was intact when it was passed to you, so what happened between you picking it up and me finding it in the stores? Tell me that!"

"Nina," he crooned, changing tack, "I wouldn't damage a historical document. It's just not in my make-up, you know that."

"I thought I knew you," she retorted, her eyes blazing with anger, "but it seems I don't. Why did you do it George? To throw researchers off the scent?"

"No…I…"

"To keep me from finding the tomb and the necklace?"

"No…Nina…you've got this all wrong."

At that, George glanced away, a tell Nina knew from the years she had worked with him. He was lying and she had just figured out why.

"Oh my God. You were going to take the jewels for yourself."

"No, it wasn't like that!"

"Wasn't it? What was it like then George? Go on, tell me. You've as good as admitted it, so tell me."

George looked grim. He could no longer look his best archaeologist in the eye and instead found the surface of his desk more interesting.

"I had no choice," he muttered.

"What? I can't hear you."

"I had no choice," he repeated, saying it louder and looking up at her. He caught her accusatory look and was ashamed. "I owe people some money. My wife has thrown me out, the kids don't want to know me and I'm living out of my car. I had no choice. I thought I could get a good price, pay off my debts and have some left over to buy myself somewhere decent to live. When I saw the last pages of the diary showed where the tomb was, I thought it would be so easy to just go there and take the necklace… then you got in the way with your crazy idea for an expedition."

"You stopped the Board backing me, didn't you?" she said barely able to breathe. "How could you do this to me George?"

"I'm sorry. I'm in trouble and… Nina let's do this together and split the profit then you'll be able to do whatever you like!" he said eagerly. "We don't need to tell anyone. It'll be our secret."

"How dare you even suggest that!" she yelled.

There was an awkward silence. Then George spoke: "We can't just leave it there. What if someone else gets it?"

"They won't."

"How do you know?"

"Because I pieced the clues together and with the help of Jay Reynolds found the tomb and the necklace." She decided to leave out the part about the fake jewels.

"You found the necklace? Where is it?"

"Safe."

"Can I see it?"

"Are you kidding me? After what you just admitted to? There's no way I'd let you within an inch of it. Besides, Jay's taking it over to the Spanish embassy as we speak. It'll be up to them what they want to do with it."

"What happens now? Are you going to report me? Please don't report me Nina. I can't afford to lose this job."

Nina looked at him without pity.

"No, I don't have enough actual evidence to report you, George. It's my word against yours."

He sighed with relief.

"I won't report you, but you're going to do something for me."

"What is it? Anything!"

"Hand in your notice."

"What? I can't do that!"

"It's either that or I tell the entire archaeological world what you've done. Try getting a new job after that."

"They'll never believe you."

"Do you really want to take that chance?"

"I suppose not," he said, flustered.

"Have a think about what you want to do," said Nina making for the door. "You have until tomorrow to make up your mind. In the meantime, I don't want to see your face again."

She flounced out of his office, slamming the door behind her.

Nina's heart was still going ten to the dozen when she hailed a black cab outside the museum. She had arranged to meet Jay back at her flat once he had handed the jewels over to the correct authorities. They had photographed the necklace and prised the fakes out of their settings before placing the necklace and the real gems inside the shoebox.

"I hope they don't ask too many questions," she told Jay before giving him a kiss goodbye.

"As far as they'll be concerned we found it in this state. The tomb had obviously been entered by tomb raiders and they had been disturbed as they tried to take the jewels. End of story," he said confidently.

That had been three hours ago. She got into the taxi and gave him her address hoping that the American would be there to greet her. He had assured her he would be fine, but Nina was afraid something had gone wrong, that he would have been arrested for entering a tomb without the proper permissions.

She reached home 20 minutes later and climbed the stairs to her flat. As she approached, she saw the familiar form of her lover standing at her door ringing her bell.

"Jay!" she called with relief as she ran up to greet him. She threw herself into his arms and hugged him tight.

"Hey, steady," he said laughing. "Anyone would think I'd just got out of jail or something."

"I missed you, that's all," she said getting her key out of her bag and inserting it in the lock.

"How did it go?" they both said as the door opened. "You go first," Nina laughed.

"It was fine," said Jay. "I told the Spanish ambassador we stumbled upon the cave after going for a walk along the beach. We were interested to find out where it led and we found the tomb. They believed me," he said incredulously as they walked down the hallway. "I had to write up a short report, sign a couple of things and that was that. They shook my hand and told me to be sure to thank you too." He opened her living room door and ushered her in. "So, what about you? Did George confess?"

"Eventually," she said suddenly exhausted from the confrontation. She threw herself on the sofa. "I gave him an ultimatum: leave or I tell all. How can anyone trust him again?"

"You can't," said Jay with a sly look on his face. He moved closer to her and sat down. Nina gave him a puzzled look.

"What are you up to?" she asked.

"Well," he said gently running his fingers up her arm. "Now

that we've found the necklace and returned it to the Spanish, and you've confronted George... Now you have another couple of days left of your leave I thought that maybe we could spend some real quality time together."

"How do you mean?" she teased. "Like going to see the sights?"

His eyes softened as he smiled.

"I don't need to see the sights," he murmured as he gently pulled her closer so that he could nuzzle her ear. Electric shocks whizzed up and down her body as he caressed her neck. "I have all I want right here."

He kissed her passionately and Nina knew that nothing was going to ever part them. She returned his ardour letting him know that he was hers and she was his. As his hands moved down to her breasts, Nina suddenly stood up.

"What's wrong?" he asked surprised by her reaction.

"Nothing," she said with a smile. "I just thought we would be better going somewhere more comfortable, that's all."

She held out her hand to him. He took it and together they sauntered to her bedroom. As Nina closed her door she smiled. Life can't get any better this, she thought as she slowly unbuttoned her blouse.

THE END

Follow me:

www.danelsonauthor.com   https://danelsonauthor.com/
Twitter: @danelsonauthor   https://twitter.com/danelsonauthor
Instagram: dawnnelsonauthor
Goodreads: D A Nelson https://www.goodreads.com/author/show/1351494.D_A_Nelson
Facebook: www.facebook.com/authordanelson/
Amazon Central: amazon.com/author/danelson

Contact me:
Email: dawn@danelsonauthor.com

If you loved this book, you'll love...

The Jacobite's Share

D A NELSON

CHAPTER ONE

THE sun drove through the chink in the curtains like a hot knife through butter and prodded her eyes. Nina grimaced and turned over, shielding herself from the sharp rays. Surely it wasn't morning already? She had only just gotten off to sleep. Reluctantly, she opened her eyes and peered out over the expanse of her empty bed. Her pale blue bedroom was still rela-tively neat despite her having discarded her clothes on top of the chest of drawers when she got back from the pub last night.

Oh Jesus! How much cheap booze had she drunk? Too much, going by the dryness of her mouth and the pounding head-ache building at her temples. She sniffed and caught the odour of stale white wine. Oh God I stink! Why had she listened to Gracie and gone out? On a 'school night' as well! She sighed. Admittedly it had been a good night, but she was never going to drink alcohol again. Not ever.

She wondered at the time and reached for her mobile phone

from the bedside table. She saw it was just gone 6.30am but she did not have to get up yet. Bliss. Another half an hour under the cosy covers – if that bloody sun would just go away. She turned around to where the rays were slicing through the curtains and considered getting up to sort them. But the hangover already had her in its grip, so she pulled the duvet over her head and closed her eyes again. Maybe if I pretend I'm not here, I won't have to get up and go to work, she thought. And it seemed like a good plan… Until her noisy housemate burst in.

"Good morning! Merry Sunshine! Time to get up, you have work to go to!" Gracie trilled as she breezed into the room, her furry slippers swishing lightly across the carpet. Nina ignored her, keeping her eyes tight shut and her body as still as she could under the protection of the bed covers. She lamented ever thinking that sharing a flat with an early riser was a good idea.

"I know you're in there, Nina. I know you are awake. Come on, it's six-thirty! Time to get up!"

Nina heard her place a mug of – she inhaled the aroma – coffee on the bedside table, but still she did not move or make a sound.

"Nina?" there was a hint of concern in Gracie's voice. "Nina?" A hand roughly shook her shoulder and another began to remove the duvet.

"What?" Nina groaned as she yanked the duvet out of Gracie's hand and pulled it back around her. "Go away. I'm still sleeping. I'm tired. I'm hung-over thanks to you dragging me out last night and I deserve five minutes extra, no, a whole half hour extra. Besides, I've got ages yet. Leave me alone, Gracie, please."

"Excuse me!" Gracie said hands on hips, "but I hardly 'dragged' you out. I didn't force you to go to the pub and I cer-tainly didn't force you to down one-and-a-half bottles of Chardonnay."

Nina peeped out from the bedclothes. "Did I really drink that much?"

"It might have been two bottles. Yes, it was more like two bottles. No wonder you were drunk."

"I drank two bottles by myself?"

"Yes."

"You didn't have any?"

"I was on the beer, remember?"

"No." Nina pulled the blanket over her head again and groaned. She felt awful.

"Come on, up you get," Gracie said again.

"How are you so sparky at this time in the morning? Especially after a night out like we had last night?" Nina wanted to know. Faint memories were beginning to surface. Oh God, did they really sing 'I Will Survive' during the pub karaoke? Shit.

"Because I didn't have anywhere as near as much as you drank, my girl," Gracie said sitting down on the bottom of the bed. "You were drinking as if it was going out of fashion."

"I've had a hard week," Nina said. Even as she said it, she knew it wasn't strictly correct. Work had been busy, but she had coped. The truth was that she was missing Jay and last night was her way of cheering herself up. And boy had she cheered herself up! She was paying for it now.

"He's coming back you know," her flatmate said. Nina peeked out from under the blanket.

"I'm sure I don't know who you mean," she muttered before going back into hiding. She was safe under her covers. Nothing could bother her here. She took another quick peek at her friend to see Gracie giving her a look like she definitely didn't believe her. Nina had been in a state of utter depression since Jay had returned to the States nearly three weeks ago. They had kept in touch via texts and Skype, but it wasn't enough for her. It wasn't just that he wasn't there, it was the fact that while she knew her feelings for him, she wasn't 100% sure that now the handsome American had gone home he would continue feeling the same for her. She was pining for him and Gracie wasn't about to let that happen

"Are you going to get up or what?"

"What!" Nina replied. Hands grabbed the duvet and pulled it

right off. Cool air hit Nina's bare arms and legs and she pulled her nightshirt down to cover her thighs.

"Nina, get up, this is ridiculous," Gracie scolded. "He's just a guy. There are loads more out there, you know. Plus, he'll be back."

But he wasn't just a guy to Nina. He was the man who had been through a perilous adventure with her, who had been there when she had discovered a priceless Roman necklace and had comforted her when she thought they were both going to die. As well as being an archaeologist like herself, Jay was smart, handsome and he loved her. They had a real connec-tion, one she had never felt with anyone else before and it was horrible being without him. She felt like a major part of her was missing. She hoped he was feeling it too.

"Do I have to drag you out of that bed by the ankles?" Gracie threatened. She was standing now and her hands were back on her hips. A stern look was on her face and Nina could see she meant business.

"Alright, bossy knickers, I'm up, I'm up!" Nina said sitting up and grabbing her duvet back off Gracie and placing it over her legs that were, despite it being summer, decidedly chilly. She scowled at her friend, who laughed and picked up Nina's mug of coffee. Gracie then presented it to her with all the pomp and flourish of a royal lackey.

"Get that down you, m'lady," Gracie said, her green eyes twinkling with mirth. "That'll soon put hairs on your chest!" Nina was never good in the morning without the stimulation only caffeine could provide and Gracie knew it.

Nina gingerly took a sip of the instant coffee and, closing her eyes, sighed with pleasure. Oh, that was so much better. The dryness of her mouth began to go and her head didn't feel quite as woolly as it had several minutes before. She opened her eyes again and smiled at Gracie. Okay, she could do this, she could get up and face the world.

"Ah, the real Nina Esposito has finally arrived," Gracie joked. "Good?" She added nodding to the coffee.

"Yes, very," Nina replied. "Just what I needed," she added. Then she said: "Why did you get me up so early this morn-ing Gracie? I could have had another half an hour at least."

"Well, funny you should say that," her flatmate replied. "Wait here!" With the excitement of a dog with its ball, Gracie departed the bedroom and returned a minute later carrying a beautiful bunch of flowers. There was a card sticking out of the top, which Gracie whipped out and handed to Nina. "This just arrived for you."

"At this time of the morning? Jeez, they're working early."

"I know! Anyway, I thought you'd want to see it immediately." Gracie danced from foot to foot whilst Nina read the card. "Well? Who's it from? Is it from Jay? Or have you got a new admirer?"

"Is it from him?" Gracie continued, too excited to wait whilst her friend read.

Nina opened the envelope and slid out the card. "It is!" she cried excitedly.

"What does he say? When is he coming back? Can you read me the juicy bits?"

Nina took a breath and began to read: "Am flying in tonight! Will call on arrival. Got something important to speak to you about. Love Jay. P.S. Any chance you could pick me up from the airport?"

"Well that was short and sweet," Nina muttered.

"Not the most romantic of cards," Gracie agreed. She sniffed the flowers before handing them over to her friend. Nina looked puzzled and a little worried.

"What do you think he wants to speak to me about? It's all a bit mysterious. Why didn't he just say?" she added passing Gracie the note.

Gracie read it carefully. Then a smile spread over her face. "Oh my God! Of course!" she replied, eyes shining. "Don't you know what this means?"

"No," Nina said with a shrug. She took another sip of coffee. Her head was still a little fuzzy and she hoped it would clear before she went to work. "Maybe he's moving over here, maybe he's finally got a full-time job over here." Jay had been looking for a couple of months, but hadn't found anything permanent.

"No, I think it's more than that!" her room-mate squeaked.

Nina looked at her quizzically. Gracie could get excited over the opening of a bottle of milk, but she had never seen her this animated before.

"Like what?"

"Like him asking you to marry him!" Gracie squealed. The high-pitched tone caused Nina to wince.

"I don't think so," she said, "we've only been together a few weeks. It's far too early for that. Besides, I don't think Jay is the marrying type." Which only leaves the alternative, she thought.

"He is! I'm sure of it!" Gracie went on. "Why else would he fly out here with barely any notice? He's going to propose! Oh, you'll make a beautiful bride!" she gushed.

"Now hold on just a minute!" Nina said trying to pour water over the fire of Gracie's enthusiasm. Her stomach flipped. The last time anyone had wanted to talk to her about 'something important' she had found herself unceremoniously dumped. But what if Gracie was right? Did she want to marry Jay? Could she see herself as his wife? Would she say 'yes' if he asked? It would be really nice to be asked, but she wasn't sure she was the marrying type either. What if he wanted to have kids? She wasn't sure she did. And could she really, truly trust him? Last year, he had gazumped her on the sale of a Roman bottle. Despite finding herself in love with the man, it still smarted that he had done that. She shook her head, but he had explained all that, it had been a mistake. Oh, she was getting ahead of herself! He was probably coming over to break up with her. Or not. Her head began to hurt! I'm not one of those women who need a man in her life to feel worthy, she thought to herself. I'm not. If that's what it is, I'll just deal with it.

"Nina!" Gracie's voice broke through her thoughts.

"What? Sorry I was miles away."

"Thinking about your wedding?"

"No, he's not coming to ask me to marry him," Nina said firmly. "That won't be what it's about. We're still just getting to know each other. It's way too early."

"But what else can it be?" Gracie wailed. "Admit it, there's nothing else it could be! I just know it! Oh, I can't wait until your wedding. I can help you plan. It'll be great. Can I be a bridesmaid?"

"Gracie! Hold your horses! We don't know what he wants to speak to me about yet," Nina smiled. "He could be coming to tell me it's over."

Gracie looked down at the note again. "No, that's not it. He was too loved up the last time he was here. Besides if he wanted to break up with you, he'd do it over the phone or text, like Dave the Pilot did to me. Why would he fly in from the States to do that? Nope. He's flown halfway across the world to ask the woman he loves for her hand."

"I wish I had your confidence," Nina replied knowing full well that it was exactly the type of thing Jay would do. He was too much of a gentleman to dump her by text. "Anyway, I'm not going to know for sure until I see him!"

She took the note and carefully folded it back into the little envelope, slipping it back into the bouquet. She fingered the delicate blooms. He had sent her a beautiful bouquet of summer flowers, including peach roses, her favourite. Why would he do that if he was going to dump her? That didn't make sense. Then again, Jay hadn't always made sense to Nina.

"What time do you think he'll get here?" asked Gracie.

"This evening. I suppose he'll text me the details later."

"Well my girl that gives you plenty of time to do some prep before you pick him up. Come on, into the bathroom with you. We've got a fair bit of work to do before you're suitable to be seen. I mean, when was the last time you had your bikini line waxed?"

"Hey!" Nina objected. That was just a bit too personal. "And what do you mean by 'us'? I am perfectly capable of getting myself ready," she added, horrified at the thought of Gracie going anywhere near her – let alone her bikini line.

"Don't worry, I have no intention of going anywhere near your hairy bits!" Gracie laughed. "However, I do have a really nice face mask you can have and I'm willing to give your nails a French manicure. I may even help you with your hair later... for a small price!"

"And what's that?"

"I want to be the first one you tell," Gracie smiled.

"Tell what?"

"About his proposal, dafty!"

"He's not going to propose Gracie! I wish you would stop saying that!"

"He will when I've finished with you," Gracie went on as she followed Nina down the narrow hallway, her slippers mak-ing a swishing noise on the old brown carpet. "Ooh! You can borrow my new dress. It's got oomph in all the right places and I've got shoes to match. The colour will really suit you and I've got a really nice lipstick..."

At the bathroom door, Nina blocked Gracie's attempt to enter.

"This is where you leave me to get on with it," she laughed.

"But I'm coming to help you look irresistible!" Gracie wailed.

"Well unless you can pee for me or you want to scrub my back, I'd suggest you wait until I'm ready for your help."

Gracie blushed. "Okay."

"I'll give you a shout when I'm ready for my facial," Nina assured her before slipping into their small bathroom and closing the door.

Nina reached for the bath taps and turned them on. As she waited for the old plastic bath to fill, she brushed her teeth at the sink only too aware of the fluttering of nervous butterflies in her stomach. She looked at her reflection in the slowly steaming mirror. *There's no way he's going to ask me to marry him; Gracie is being silly*, she thought. *It's way too early for that. He's not the marrying type anyway.* He was already in his 30s and still hadn't walked down the aisle. *There was no way he was going to propose, no way. So, what is it he wants to see me about?*

She felt her stomach drop.

Stop it! she scolded herself. *Stop thinking the worse!*

She spat into the bowl, turned the tap and watched the foamy white gloop swirl down the plughole.

She glanced at her face again in the mirror. There was a worried look in her eyes.

Get a grip woman! she chided. *Stop thinking about it. No point worrying about it until you know for sure!* She replaced her toothbrush in its holder in the little vanity cupboard she shared with Gracie. *No point at all!* But as she threw some bath salts into the steaming water and turned off the taps, she felt depressed and hopeless, as if her whole world were about to collapse. *For God's sake*, she told herself, *I should be happy. He's coming to see me tonight!*

She got into the water and savoured its warmth.

"Oh, bugger Jay!" she said aloud. "Even when you're not here, you're driving me nuts!" She sank beneath the water.

Nina emerged from the bathroom 40 minutes later red as a lobster and wrinkly as an octogenarian. With a fluffy pink towel wrapped turban-style around her long dark hair, and her favourite towelling robe on, she joined Gracie in their shabby chic living room. Gracie saw her friend's miserable expression and her own face fell.

"What's wrong?" Gracie asked, patting the sofa to encourage her friend to sit down. The sofa was old, but comfortable and matched the grey armchair sitting in the corner next to the television. The room was small, but cosy. An old gas fire-place sat opposite the sofa above which was a large mirror Gracie had picked up in an antiques market some years before. The walls, which were painted a soothing pale yellow, were adorned with framed photographs of Gracie and Nina at vari-ous events they had attended together along with some family snaps and a black and white still of the actor, Tom Hardy. Gracie had insisted that it be put up because, she explained, looking at the delectable Mr Hardy every day made her day worthwhile. Nina plonked herself down on the sofa and allowed her friend to put her arms around her.

"He's going to dump me, I know it."

"Don't be daft! You're just being paranoid," Gracie replied. "Look, I'm sorry I went a bit over the top earlier. He's prob-ably just wanting to tell you about some family news or something, that's all."

"Then why is he flying over?"

"Because he loves you and misses you and..."

"And?"

"Well he's not had it for several weeks. He must be fit to bursting by now!"

"Gracie!" said Nina in faux shock. "You're terrible!"

"But that's why you love me!" her friend laughed. "And it got you to smile!"

Nina spent a miserable day at work counting down the hours until she would be forced to become single again… or so her annoying inner voice kept telling her. She had always been un-sure about having a long-distance relationship, worried she was already in too deep with her feelings for Jay when they were so far apart so many times. There was no doubt in her mind that at some point he would get fed up with all the travel and find someone else, someone better and closer to home. She went through possible conversation scenarios all morning until she could take it no more. She grabbed her bag to pop out to her favourite café a couple of streets away and had just gotten her jacket on when she was stopped in her tracks by her boss, Dorothy Robertson.

"Have you got a minute Nina, darling?" she asked. Dorothy Robertson was Nina's new boss. A tall, pretty woman of about 30, she was dark-haired and slim, and had the accent of someone who had attended an exclusive girls' school. Since her previous boss, George, had been forced to leave the museum, Dorothy had taken over and had a habit of recommend-ing her best archaeologist for all sorts of weird and wonderful jobs.

"Yes, of course," Nina replied.

"I want you to meet someone," her boss replied. "He's down from Scotland for the week and is keen to meet you."

"Who is it?"

"Come on, I'll introduce you," Dorothy said with a smile.

Nina followed her along the corridor to her office. Larger and more lavishly furnished than Nina's, it was currently oc-cupied by a tall, handsome man in biker leathers. He was staring out of the window when they approached and turned to greet them with a dazzling smile. Dorothy giggled. She seemed a little different around this man – almost coy - and Nina wondered about their relationship. Her boss grabbed the stranger's hand and gave it a seemingly familiar squeeze.

"Nina, this is Tom MacDow and he has a possible job for you," she said, eyes twinkling with delight. Nina put out her hand and shook his outstretched hand. It was soft but firm.

"Pleased to meet you Mr MacDow," she said drinking in the sheer gorgeousness of his dark brown eyes. Like Galaxy chocolate, Gracie would have said. Nina felt a little flutter of excitement in her stomach. Tom MacDow was in his early 30s, extremely handsome and giving her a killer smile. I have a boyfriend, I have a boyfriend, Nina thought to herself as she took a seat proffered by Dorothy. Her boss sat behind her large oak desk and smiled as Tom MacDow took the other seat next to Nina. He gave her another sexy grin and Nina felt herself blush from her crown to her toes.

"So," she said looking at Dorothy, "you said Mr MacDow wanted to see me?" She looked at Tom shyly and he was still grinning.

"Tom, darling, why don't you take Nina through it?" Dorothy said.

"Of course," he said in a soft Scottish accent. "I'm from the MacDow family of Dundow Castle in Perthshire, Scotland. My brother Duncan took over as Laird when our father died three years ago and since then, with death duties and running costs, we've struggled to keep the old place going. That's where you come in, Miss Esposito."

"I do?" She couldn't see how.

"Squirrelled away somewhere within Dundow Castle, or in its grounds, is Jacobite treasure hidden there by our ancestor Angus MacDow in 1745. The family has looked over the generations, but we've never found anything. We can't pay you very much, but you'll also get room and board for the time you are there. Dorothy says you've got some annual leave com-ing up, so I wondered if you wanted to come to Scotland and help us treasure hunt?"

"I… don't… know," she said slowly. "Why me? Surely there are other people in Scotland who could help?"

"After your success with that necklace in Mallorca, I want you. According to Dorothy, you're the best."

"That necklace turned out to be a fake," she replied thinking back to a few months previously when she and Jay had dis-covered the tomb of the Roman noblewoman Aelia near Alcudia. They had found her and her fabled necklace only to have it stolen by Nina's ex-boyfriend Roberto and his billionaire boss. After she and Jay nearly lost their lives in Aelia's tomb, she didn't want to have to go through all that again.

"Yes, but you didn't know that at the time," he replied. "You found it after everyone else had given up. We need some-one with your tenacity to find our treasure and save our home."

"When you say 'treasure', what exactly are you hoping I'll find?"

Tom continued: "According to family legend, the treasure consists of gold coins and jewels sent to Bonnie Prince Char-lie from France for his campaign to return the British throne to the Stuarts. It arrived days before the Battle of Culloden. My ancestor Duncan MacDow guarded the treasure for the Prince, but when Charlie was defeated at the battle, Duncan hid it on his property to safeguard it from Government troops. He was arrested and tried as a traitor a week later. Before he died though, he sent his wife Estelle a letter with clues as to where the treasure might be hidden. The letter was lost, but we think it is still somewhere in the castle. Many family members have tried to find it but failed. We need help. We need some-one to find that letter and unravel the mystery."

Nina bit her lip and thought for a moment. It could be fun, but Jay was coming and she was hoping to persuade Doro-thy to let her have a few days off so she could spend some time with him. It was a no brainer.

"I am very tempted, I'm sorry, Mr MacDow, but I'll have to pass," she said.

"Are you sure? This could be the find of the century!" He looked at her intently, willing her to take the job. Yet despite the pleading in those gorgeous brown eyes, Nina remained firm.

"I'm sorry Mr MacDow, but I really must decline," she said.

He looked disappointed but nodded, accepting her decision. He took a business card from his wallet and handed it to her.

"If you change your mind, here's where you'll get me," he said.

"Thank you," she replied. "Is there anything else I can help you with?" He shook his head. "Well, I'll say goodbye then. And good luck finding your treasure." She stood up, shook his hand, nodded to her boss and left the office. Outside, in the corridor, she wondered if she had made the right decision. It did sound intriguing but Jay was more important to her. She needed to spend her vacation time with him not go running off to Scotland on a treasure hunt. Her heart sank. Oh God, I hope he's not coming to finish with me, she thought, I've just knocked back a job I'd normally kill for. I love Jay, I really do and I don't know what I'll do if he dumps me. Then her rational side kicked in. If he was going to end it with me, why not do it over the phone? Why spend all that time and money coming to London? She shook her head, scolding herself for being silly, and stepped out into the bright sunny morning, her head full of Jay and Jacobite treasure.

Nina stood on her tiptoes to see over the crowd at the arrivals gate in Heathrow Airport. The doors had been open for some time and there was still no sign of that tall blond American she had once loathed and now loved. He had finally texted her his flight details and now she was wondering if he would appear. Her eyes never left the arrivals doors. First through were a fat family - mum, dad and two children squeezed into stretchy jogging trousers and t-shirts, faces mottled from eating too much processed food - wheeling a groaning trolley piled high with gaudy plastic suitcases. Three younger women, tanned and laughing, all painted-on eyebrows, long glossy hair and false eyelashes, followed. A young couple, awk-wardly walking arm-in-arm as the man pulled their wheeled case, emerged after them, but still no Jay. With every opening of the door, her stomach flipped and her heart raced. Nina moved position, trying to get closer to the barrier so that she might see him first.

"Excuse me," she said squeezing past a white-haired man with a large belly and sweaty face.

"Sorry," she apologised as she accidentally trod on the exquisitely shod foot of a snotty looking older woman who looked in need of a good feed. The woman, all perfume and pursed lips, glared as Nina gave her a weak smile.

"Do you mind?" the woman snapped.

"I didn't mean to...! Oh!" And that was when, from the corner of her eye, she became aware of a tall handsome someone leaving the gate; a tall, handsome someone with blond hair and a smile that could melt the meanest heart. She looked up and her eyes locked with his. He was grinning from ear to ear and her heart sang as she smiled back and waved at him. Ges-turing frantically that she would meet him over there, ignoring the tuts of the woman, Nina squeezed through the crowd again and eventually released herself from the press of waiting relatives.

"You causing trouble again?" he chuckled as he wrapped his strong arms around her slim waist.

"Always!" she murmured as she stretched up for a kiss. His lips found hers and for one blissful moment she forgot eve-rything; her fears, her hopes, the disapproving crowd nearby. All was Jay: his lips, his strong hands around her waist, the warmth of his body, his smell. Jay's lips were soft and warm and full of yearn-ing for her as they sought and engaged with hers. She sighed contentedly.

"Get a room. That's disgusting!" she heard the po-faced woman sneer.

Jay broke from her, looked up and frowned, but Nina easily dis-tracted him with a peck on the lips. "Don't mind her," Nina said grabbing his arm and guiding him away. "People always have far too much to say for themselves. Come on, the car's in the car park."

She wanted to get him all to herself as quickly as possible. She had really missed him; missed him to the very core of her being. She slipped her hand into his and together they walked through the sliding glass doors into the cool evening air.

Jay had barely stowed his luggage into the boot of her car be-fore grabbing her again for a long and lingering kiss. He held her tightly, his lips on hers, the hard, muscular lines of his body pressed up against hers, kissing her like he hadn't seen her in a hundred years. Nina felt a thrill of excitement shoot through her body and she could feel he was just as excited at seeing her as his groin tightened and swelled against her pelvis. Well hello Jay! she thought. You have missed me after all. She let out a small moan of pleasure as his lips left hers and began exploring her neck. Oh God she had missed this! Really missed this. His touch made her body tingle and she was just relaxing into the sensation when he pulled away and held her from him. She frowned.

"I think that's about enough of that for now!" he grinned and kissed the top of her nose.

"What? I was just getting into that," she complained.

"So was I," he admitted, "but we're gathering a bit of an audience who don't look as if they approve."

Nina glanced around to see the po-faced woman and her equally stern friend throwing daggers at them. The first woman tutted loudly, threw her pinched nose into the air and walked smartly to her own car which was parked a few spaces from hers.

Nina turned her attention back to Jay, a look of wicked delight on her face.

"Oh well, how to win friends and influence people!" she joked. Jay laughed.

She smiled back, her whole body radiant with joy that he was here, with her, in the airport car park. She couldn't wait to get him into bed.

"I've really missed you," he said, suddenly serious.

"Me too! I mean I've really missed you too," she replied.

"Well, I'll be able to show you exactly how much I've missed you later," Jay said, "but for now I'm starved."

"I knew you'd be hungry after your flight, so I've got us a table at a lovely little restaurant I know. I think you'll approve. Do you want to come home and freshen up first or go straight there?"

Jay looked at her like she had two heads.

"Food first, then we can freshen up back at yours!" he smirked, waggling his eyebrows comically to make his point.

"Well, we best get you fed then. I don't want your stamina to fail you when we get 'refreshed' later.'" Nina replied. Her stomach flipped. Why was he so keen to get to the restaurant? She wondered. The doubts crept into her brain again. Was he just pretending to be happy to see her? Was he actually just waiting to get her into the restaurant to tell her it was over? It was a public place, where better to ensure she didn't create a scene?

"Heaven forbid!" he replied then he frowned. "Are you okay? You seem a bit weird."

"Me?" she said forcing a smile. "Oh, I'm fine. Really. Just can't believe you're actually here. At such short notice."

"Don't you want me here?"

"Of course, I do," she said.

"Well, that's okay then."

He gave her a quick peck on the lips and they parted, each to a different side of the car. Nina slipped into the driver's side. Jay took his place in the passenger's seat, putting the CD player on before Nina even had her seatbelt on. The dulcet tones of Caro Emerald filled the car and he hummed along. Nina started the engine and soon they were speeding towards the M4 heading for London and Nina's flat.

Forty minutes later they parked the car in Nina's lock-up. Taking his bag with him, Jay slipped his free arm around Nina's waist and gave her a squeeze.

"Lead on MacDuff!" he said. "Take me to the food place, I am so hungry I could eat you!"

Nina gave him a wolfish grin. "Down tiger!" she said.

Arm-in-arm they walked down the street towards Nina's favourite Chinese restaurant a few hundred yards away. She had booked it that morning knowing her choice would be welcomed by Jay, who also loved Eastern cuisine. The smell of orien-tal cooking hit them some metres from the building and it was on this haze of happy anticipation of a delicious meal that Nina led Jay into the restaurant. Chong's was a more traditional-style restaurant serving real Chinese food and was the fa-vourite haunt of many of the local Chinese community – always a good sign, Nina thought. It had a kind of modern vin-tage feel: on one hand it had the trimmings of a traditional Chinese restaurant with dragons, lanterns and red everywhere, but the contemporary tables and chairs were wooden and chrome. There were black and white images of film stars from the 1950s adorning the crimson walls and a massive modern chandelier hung from centre of the ceiling. It was a strange com-bination, but seemed to work. Gavin, the restaurant's owner, greeted her like an old friend and showed them to her favour-ite booth at the back. Nina slid into her seat and licked her lips. She was hungry. Gavin handed them a menu each, took their drinks order and left the two of them alone.

Nina glanced at the menu in the light of a small candle, but she closed it with a sigh and put it on the table. She knew what she was going to order. She always had the same thing. She just wished Jay would hurry up looking at the menu so they could get down to the crux of why he had suddenly decided to fly the three-and-a-half thousand miles on such short notice. She wanted to get it over with, whatever it was.

"So," she said unable to contain herself any longer, "what's the big news you have to tell me?"

DUSTING DOWN ALCUDIA

My other Books

Adults:
Everything She Wants

Children's:
DarkIsle
DarkIsle: Resurrection
DarkIsle: The Final Battle
A Children's History of Glasgow

Made in United States
North Haven, CT
27 May 2022